WHO'S YOUR DADDY

AN ACCIDENTAL PREGNANCY REVERSE HAREM ROMANCE

STASIA BLACK

ISBN-13: 978-1-63900-159-0

*To the girls who grew up crushing on *****all****** the boys in the band... ;)*

Want to read an EXCLUSIVE, FREE novella, *Indecent: a Taboo Proposal*, that is available ONLY to my newsletter subscribers, along with news about upcoming releases, sales, exclusive giveaways, and more?

Get Indecent: a Taboo Proposal

https://geni.us/SBA-nw-cont-w

When Mia's boyfriend takes her out to her favorite restaurant on their six-year anniversary, she's expecting one kind of proposal. What she didn't expect was her boyfriend's longtime rival, Vaughn McBride, to show up and make a completely different sort of offer: all her boyfriend's debts will be wiped clear. The price?

One night with her.

Trigger Warnings:

a romance with mature themes, spank!ng, breath play, daddy play, and dominance/$ubmi$$on.

1

MEETING A MAVROS TWIN

I've felt like Alice falling down the rabbit hole ever since I met the Mavros twins three months ago.

Naïve little virgin that I was. Ha!

Now look at me.

It'll be the story of the century if anyone ever finds out. I can just see the headline: *Who's Your Daddy?*

Because the thing is... we'll never know.

DNA tests are only so-so accurate when it comes to differentiating between familial relations. We'll never truly know which brother's child rests in my belly right now. Dear God. My cheeks flame. As usual.

What would Daddy say if he could see me now?

But I'm getting ahead of myself.

Let's go back to the beginning, when once upon a time, a naïve publicist walked into the office of one of Hollywood's most rich and famous at the request of a friend—an acquaintance, really.

If only I'd had any idea that was a day that would change my life forever. My hand drifts down to my ever-expanding belly.

At least I would have worn a different outfit, that was for damn sure.

~

Two months earlier

I TRIED to keep my head high and act like I belonged as I walked into the LA high rise to meet with one of the biggest stars in the industry.

Leander Mavros.

Holy crap. I was actually here to see Leander frickin' Mavros! He was only one of the hottest up and coming young actors of our generation. He already had two Emmy's under his belt. And after another critically acclaimed season of his popular Netflix thriller *Gemini*, I had no doubt there'd be a third this year.

Nope. No fangirling. I belonged here... right?

Of course you belong, Hope. Self-hype was all the rage in therapy these days. Well, that and attachment theory. But thanks to dear moms and pops, I was screwed over attachment-wise (avoidant attachment-style here *ftw*), so I might as well focus on the first. Positivity.

...and go.

You can do this!

You're a champ!

Just look at how far you've come in less than a decade!

The butterflies that had been fluttering in my stomach turned to moths, and then to mothballs, and then to spaghetti balls, and then I couldn't decide if I was hungry or just felt like throwing up.

It was true, I had been publicist to some of the hottest

young tween starlets of the last decade. I mean, just calling me a publicist was a joke. Unofficially I'd been everything from babysitter to mother-figure to confidant to those girls.

There was a reason the starlets I managed never self-imploded like so many other young stars did. I kept them on the straight and narrow. And I got them into therapy and heard a lot about it secondhand.

My most recent client, Makayla Mitchell, was starring in that big new superhero movie everyone had been talking about lately. And Destiny, my first mega client, just finished her first solo R&B tour, selling out tickets in arenas worldwide. It was success beyond all of our wildest dreams.

And the fact that I'd helped not one but two stars navigate the industry through their awkward teenage years—when so many of their peers had flamed out with drugs, sex scandals, and predatory parents or other family members—apparently, someone had noticed. The fact that I was here today was testament to that fact. To be here, in the lobby of one of LA's most exclusive talent agencies to meet with either Leander or his twin brother Janus? It was a big deal.

My contact Milo hadn't said much over the phone, just that they had some publicity problem they needed outside assistance with.

Other than that, I had no clue what it was about. I always had my ear to the ground when it came to the inner circle gossip and the only buzz about Leander lately was surrounding his first big blockbuster movie coming out in a week. It was his big break from TV into movies. So far reviews had been good.

But what if it wasn't Leander I met today, but Janus, his twin brother? Janus didn't act anymore, but he co-managed his brother's career with Milo, their longtime best friend. All three had been child stars together. The twins co-played a famously adored little kid on a beloved sitcom in the early aughts.

As teenagers, both twins had been heartthrobs. So many girls at my school had pictures of them in their lockers. Not me, naturally. I'd been lucky enough that my freaky-religious parents even let me *go* to public high school.

I took a deep breath as I pushed the *up* button on the elevator. I couldn't think about any of that now. It had been years and years ago. Lord knew I was worlds away from the girl I'd been as that shy, sheltered little teenager.

As the elevator doors slid open and I stepped inside, I glanced at myself in the full-length mirrored walls. The lift of the elevator made my stomach swish, and I took a moment to really examine myself.

My hair was in low pigtails and while yes, I was wearing a tight shirt that my mother would have been completely *aghast* at, baring cleavage and all... I was also wearing overalls.

I mean, they were cute overalls... but they were still overalls.

It was the kind of outfit that fit in perfectly at the Nickelodeon or Pixar studios where most of my previous clients hung out.

Milo had made it sound so urgent on the phone, I hadn't thought to change before swinging over. But now my cheeks heated because good Lord, had I really changed that much since I was a teenager after all? Yes, I had traveled the globe with my clients, and attended some of the biggest movie premieres in the world, and my contact list was drool-worthy...

But standing here, riding the elevator to meet with the person named *People's* "Sexiest Man Alive" and looking at myself in the mirror?

With my bright pink round cheeks, I still *looked* about

fifteen. Dear God, there was no denying that I was a twenty-seven-year-old virgin, was there?

The elevator pinged and the doors popped open before I was ready.

And standing there in front of me, in tall and undeniable godly glory was—

"H-hi," I said, then wanted to pinch myself for my damn stutter kicking in. Usually I was never starstruck. I'd trained myself not to be. I'd found that if you focused on a celebrity's eyebrows when talking to them, they seemed just like anybody else.

But I just hadn't been prepared.

I didn't know which twin I was staring up at—Leander or Janus—but he was broad-chested, and bigger than he looked on TV. I mean, his chest really went *on and on*. He was wearing a grey thermal that was stretched taut by his muscles but still looked really, really soft at the same time—

"Are you lost?"

"Huh?" I jerked my attention back where he was standing in the foyer the elevator had opened into. He was looking at his phone but had glanced up at me, clearly dismissing me as he went back to whatever was capturing his attention on his phone.

"Oh. Oh no." I stood up straight and shrugged my overly large bag over my shoulder. "No, I'm supposed to be here."

Now it was time for the intimidating, tall sexy giant to blink, when he finally took another glance up from his phone. "Supposed to be here?"

Just then, rescue came in the form of Milo Pappas from around the corner. Milo was not only the twins' best friend, he was their head of security/manager. As a fellow behind-the-scener, we ran in the same circles. He'd always seemed competent and kind to me, in an industry that thrived on corrupt and self-serving. Not to mention that he came in a similarly giant Greek package—

Oh shit, did I really just think *giant Greek package?*

I was going to hell. It was official now. The fires were coming. My cheeks flamed hot and I only barely stopped myself from fanning them.

I will not fangirl and faint in front of Leander-or-Janus Mavros. I will not *fangirl and faint in front of—*

"Seriously, you shouldn't be on this floor. Do I need to call secu—" Leander-or-Janus started gruffly, only giving me more than a cursory glance for the first time.

His dark gaze paused on my face as he looked me up and down.

Our eyes connected.

It sounded stupid, but it felt physical. Maybe it was just the idiotic stray thought I'd had a moment ago about *giant Greek packages*, but I felt that gaze like a sizzle striking the back of my spine. Right down to the tailbone. And echoing around straight to my—

Milo finished Leander-or-Janus's sentence with a wide smile and open arms. "Security? Nonsense. Janus, this is Hope Robins. She's the publicist we've been waiting for. Come in, come in."

Milo ushered me forward just as a curious twinkle lit in Janus's eye.

"We've been expecting you. You're late." And then in a deep bass voice, he finished. "I don't like tardiness."

2

THE PROPOSITION

"Ignore him," Milo said, ushering me in warmly with a hand at the small of my back. It was a move that Janus didn't miss noticing, I saw.

The meatballs in my stomach suddenly turned back into butterflies. Dear Lord, I was gonna get vertigo at this rate. Why on God's green earth was I reacting to this man this way when I never did to other celebrities?

I glanced over at Janus, inhaling at what it felt like just to be near a man of such... *magnetism*. Janus hadn't even acted in over a decade and wasn't technically a celebrity anymore. And it wasn't even about that. He just had this potent... *energy*.

Milo led us into what looked more like a hotel room than any office I'd ever seen, an open concept space with a little sunken area full of couches in the middle of the room and a full kitchen off to the side. Mid-morning sunlight filtered through floor to ceiling shades. It lit up the modern apartment done in sleek blacks, grays, and creams.

Milo took a seat on the edge of one couch, gesturing with his hands as he started talking. "We're so glad you've come, aren't we, Janus? I was just telling Janus here how I knew what we needed, I knew just who to call. Hope! Hope would give us hope, wasn't that exactly what I was telling you? And voila! Here she is! In the flesh."

At the word *flesh*, Janus's eyes flicked up and down my body again. I felt my cheeks flush. Good Lord. Didn't he know that was... well... it was *uncouth*. Even if he had done so relatively discreetly. I hadn't missed the flare of interest I'd registered in his eyes before he'd glanced away again, walking towards the bar opposite the kitchen.

Though he didn't pour himself anything to drink. Instead, he suddenly turned around and cut off Milo's warm stream of consciousness by asking, "So is it Mrs. Robins... or *Ms.* Robins?"

The way the register of his deep voice lingered on the *Ms.* in that phrase was truly obscene.

"It's M-m-m," I squeezed my eyes shut, cheeks heating in the hell of my stammer, "M-m-m-m— *I'm single*," I finally finished with an expulsion of breath.

There was an awkward moment of silence and I was sure that my cheeks were overheated jars of tomato sauce about to explode.

"O-kaaay," Milo laughed, then clapped his hands. "Why don't we get down to it?"

Dear God, why did everything sound like sexual innuendo right now? I had a problem. I sat down hastily on a couch across from Milo. Smoothing my damp palms down the denim of my overalls didn't help, and when I felt Janus's eyes on me again, I balled them into fists.

I cleared my throat and tried to pull on all my professional training. For my sanity, though, I looked away from Janus and addressed Milo.

"You said you had some kind of PR emergency? Where's your normal publicist? Why aren't they helping you?"

"Well," Milo hedged, his open face suddenly clouding.

"Are you sure she's right for this?" Janus asked, walking lazily back towards us. "She looks about ten."

I blanched, my mouth dropping open. Did he really just say that?

Milo swore under his breath. "Jesus, usually it's Leander who's the asshole. What's with you today?"

Janus glared at him. "I don't know. Maybe it's because the last publicist we brought in fucked us over so badly."

Okay, they had my attention now.

As if they'd ever lost it. The Mavros twins were notoriously hot when they were pissed off. It was just one of the reasons Leander's TV show *Gemini* was such a hit. I had a hard time looking away from his sculpted face. I had to keep forcing my eyes back to Milo so I wasn't caught staring.

"What happened?" I asked, proud I'd managed it without any stuttering. The malady only hit when I was either extremely nervous or extremely excited. I couldn't tell which I was right now, though I suspected it was some screwed up mix of both.

Milo and Leander just shared a dark look. Then Milo finally spoke up. "If she's going to help us, we have to tell her."

"Fine, but make her sign an NDA first."

Milo rolled his eyes but nodded. "Naturally."

"Of course I'm happy to," I hurried to say, then reassured them, "I always keep my client's information strictly confidential. But I understand how important paperwork is."

Milo picked up an iPad from a side table by the couch where he was sitting and handed it over. I signed with my finger and handed it back. Then I looked at the two men expectantly. "So how can I help you today?"

I expected them to come right out with it, but instead, Janus finally sat down on the couch corner next to mine, so that we were almost seated side by side. With him so near, I was hit by the male scent of him—not overwhelming, but definitely present. Aftershave? Cologne?

"I take it you're familiar with my brother's career?" he asked.

I nodded, trying to keep my cool while also maintaining eye contact. I'd chatted easily with Oscar winners before. I could do this. "And yours," I said politely.

Janus smirked. "Such as it was. He's the star now. I'm just in the shadows. Spotlight doesn't agree with me."

I wasn't sure how to respond to that—even though I had a lot to say on the topic of child stars, considering my place in the industry. It wasn't as if adolescence had been kind to either Mavros twin. Like so many child stars who didn't have a strong support system, the twins had spiraled in their mid-to-late teens.

Both of them had quite publicly engaged in every sort of debauchery they could find. There were pictures of them with powder on their noses. One or the other of them making out with some starlet or another, often with arms around two women at once. Usually stumbling out of whatever club he was too young to have been in in the first place.

The last straw was a drunk driving incident when Janus drove into someone's *house*. That was when Janus had stopped acting and only Leander continued on to fame as an adult.

But it wasn't like I was going to say any of that to the man's face. Or ask any of the thousand and one unanswered questions of our generation: Why had only one twin continued to act and the other quit? Janus never took interviews and Leander was notoriously tight-lipped about his twin.

But I didn't want to screw this up before we'd even gotten started. More than anyone, I knew how important it was to respect a public person's privacy.

"So. The situation?" I prompted again.

Milo tried to start talking but Janus just shook his head, cutting him off. "First, my brother. You know his career. Have you seen his movies?"

I frowned. "Has he made other movies? I thought this one was his big break into film."

Janus narrowed his eyes. "So you didn't see his couple indie films?" He reeled off some titles I didn't know. One of them was vaguely familiar, maybe I'd heard it on some entertainment news show or from buzz in the community.

I blinked and glanced at Milo. Why was this starting to feel like an interrogation? "Uh, sorry, no. Do I need to? Is whatever happened related to one of—"

"Janus, stop it. I told you, she's a good girl."

I looked back and forth between Milo and Janus, and Milo obviously must have seen the confusion on my face.

"He's trying to see if you're hardcore," Milo explained, as if that was any explanation at all.

"Hardcore?"

"If you're some kind of hardcore fangirl."

I laughed out loud at that. And then realized when no one else did that Milo was being serious. What the hell?

Milo was a friend, but even that was kind of a stretch. We only sort of knew each other. I was about three seconds from grabbing my purse and making tracks. "Look, you called *me* here. Please stop disrespecting my professional reputation with this crap. Either I can help you or I can't. But stop wasting my time."

And I did reach for my purse. If only because I was annoyed at how close they were getting to the truth. Getting out of here might be best for my sanity anyway. This clearly wasn't a gig for me.

"You're the one who showed up to an interview looking like you're in junior high," Janus shot back.

My face flamed. "Because he said it was an emergency. So sorry I didn't stop home to change, your majesty. And what are you talking about, job interview? I thought this was just a consult on a specific situation?" I looked to Milo for confirmation.

But it was Janus who clarified. "Well, now it's an interview. Here's our problem. A woman is threatening to go to the tabloids with a story about Leander. About both of us actually."

"Okay," I frowned, not getting the point. "Surely you must get that kind of thing all the time. What makes this one any different?"

Janus drew his hands together, interlocking his fingers as he leaned forward, elbows on knees. "Well, this situation is a little more delicate because the allegations she's making are... *true.*"

I blinked and sucked in a little breath, not sure if I wanted to hear the answer to my next question but determined to barrel on anyway. "And what exactly is it she's alleging you two did to her?" —at the same time praying, *please don't let it be something that will make me hate you.*

Still, in no way could I have prepared myself for what he said next.

"She's going to go to the press and tell them that my brother and I like to fuck the same woman at once. And she has evidence that will prove it."

I swallowed hard. "Oh. Evidence?"

"A video recording."

"Oh."

He nodded. "Oh."

My mind began spinning. "Well, with deep fakes, any video can be manipulated—"

"It's not a deep fake. She must have set up her phone to record before we fucked."

Dear Lord, he just admitted it so casually.

He and his brother—

Both at once?

How did that even work? My mind stalled out. I couldn't even understand the mechanics of it. There was only one hole down there. Then I felt my eyes widen even further. Well, I mean *technically* there were two. Had she—whoever this *she* was—had she taken them both at the same time, one in each, or—?

"Ms. Robins?"

"Mmm hmm," I said, looking back into the gorgeous face of the man who'd just admitted sharing a woman with his twin brother. I blinked rapidly then reached down to yank out a little notebook from my purse to keep him from seeing my flaming face.

Okay, Hope. Time to refocus and do your job. I could let my brain wrap around it later. I clicked my pen, ready to start jotting down notes. "And who is this woman? Someone you came across at a club? Where did you find her?"

Janus took just a beat before answering. "She was our former publicist. The one we hope you'll be replacing."

3

...AND THEN I MEET THE OTHER ONE

I was still trying to process what I just heard. The twins had an affair with their last publicist. *Both twins. At once.*

My mind still spun. I tried to remember if I ever saw the woman around at any events I attended. But for the life of me I couldn't recall what she looked like, or even her name.

"Who the fuck is this?"

My head jerked up at hearing Janus's voice from across the room. Except it wasn't Janus, obviously. He was still sitting right beside me.

Oh my God, oh my God, it was—

Leander Mavros. Movie star. Mogul. Rich and famous beyond all imagining.

I had assumed he wasn't here. From rumors I'd heard, Janus sometimes acted as a body-double, so I'd figured Janus was taking the meeting *for* his brother.

I'd only just gotten my heart rate used to one Greek god taking up all the air in the room, and now there were *two of them*??

And why was Leander... staring at me like that?

He wasn't staring at my boobs or anything rude—he was

looking at my face, though his eyes did do a quick up and down scan, then he was back to squinting at me, a frozen, confused look on his features.

"Meet our new publicist," Milo said at the same time Janus said, "Just someone we're interviewing."

Uh...

"No," Leander said.

A single syllable.

Then turned as if he was going to go.

"Excuse me?" I said, embarrassed when it came out more like a squeak. And then I just got mad. Mad at how this meeting was going. Mad at my stupid, overheated cheeks that gave away my embarrassment for all to see. And mad that I'd been put in this position at all. For some godlike movie star to take one look down his nose at me and then dismiss me.

I hadn't gotten where I was in this industry by letting important men walk all over me. I might rep teeny boppers, but I had to deal day in day out with the gatekeepers of the industry who were still annoyingly, overwhelmingly, and monochromatically *male.*

"Leander!" Milo had stood up outraged. "This is Hope Robins, an extremely talented publicist and fixer—"

But I put a hand out. I didn't need anyone defending me.

"Start at the beginning," I interrupted. "You said there's a tape. Has it leaked yet? It's likely just a matter of time so we need to start building multiple action plans for each scenario. We'll have to be ready to change with the evolving situation. You're men, so a sex tape won't be as bad as if you were female, but the fact that both of you are in it together—"

I sucked in a breath, daring to glance at each of the three faces in the room. Milo looked eager, Janus seemed to be listening, Leander was brooding and bored-looking, so I finished quickly, "—obviously lends a salaciousness that could give this thing a longer news life-cycle than you might want. We don't want an Armie Hammer fiasco on our hands."

"It's hardly fantasies of cannibalism!" Milo reacted, gesturing even more passionately with his hands than usual.

"And we didn't hurt her," Leander growled. "She was the one who came to us begging."

"Is she saying differently?" I asked politely.

"Thankfully, no," Milo said, sitting back down and running a hand through his hair. "You can see that plainly enough on the tape that she's a... well, an enthusiastic participant. But when things were broken off, she didn't take it well."

"She was shit at her job," Leander said, glass clinking as he poured himself a whiskey. "She thought fucking us meant she'd keep it even if she slacked off all the time, but that's not how it works. It was explained repeatedly to her, so I hear."

"Was there infidelity?" Then I paused. "I mean, did it even work like that?" I didn't know how the rules of "situations" with more than one person worked.

"I assure you, Miss Robins," Leander said, walking towards the window and looking out, glass in hand, "that unlike whatever tabloid image you have of us, we're careful who we fuck. And we only do it one woman at a time."

We?

Dear God, did that mean they always slept with women... together?

"What my brother's trying to say," Janus sounded irritated at his brother's bluntness, "was that there was infidelity, but it wasn't us. By the end, I found out Geena was sleeping with anything that moved. And she'd gone on from coke to meth. She was screwing up every booking."

"She knew the rules and she broke them," Milo reiterated.

Leander turned from the window, glaring at his brother and Milo. "If you two had told me what was going on sooner, maybe we could have stopped all this before it got out of hand. I'm not some piece of fine fucking china."

I lifted an eyebrow but kept my thoughts to myself.

The truth was, a lot of my clients were like this when I first got to them. Messy family dynamics were usually a given when you were talking about a client with millions and millions and *millions* of dollars on the line. I wouldn't be able to unwind all the tangled vines of the situation until I really dug in, but I was starting to get a hazy outline.

"What kind of paperwork did you have her sign?" I asked. "What are we working with here?"

"Yes, yes," Milo said, perking up. "We did everything by the book as far as HR at his talent agency. I disclosed that Leander was sleeping with a contract employee and they both signed liability waivers."

"I did?" Leander asked, sounding genuinely surprised.

Janus waved it away. "I signed it for you."

"I didn't hear that, and it never leaves this room," I jumped in to say quickly. "So she has no leg to stand on legally? Not that it always matters, but it's a start."

Janus nodded. "Some of her fuck-ups on the job were so public, we had endless grounds to fire her. But if she goes to the press, that's not what they'll care about."

"Nope," I agreed. "All they'll hear is the salacious bit."

"So far Geena's only *threatening* to go to the press," Milo said, like he was trying to be hopeful. "She hasn't actually done it yet. Maybe it's just a bluff."

I jotted down more notes on my pad as I continued asking questions. "Is she making demands? Money? If she's trying to extort you, we can use that against her."

Milo tipped his head back and forth. "Not exactly. She doesn't want money. She wants..." He looked back and forth between Leander and Janus.

"What?" I asked. "Don't hold back now."

"What if we did let her back in?" Leander asked in a tone I couldn't read.

"Wha—?" Milo started, outraged, and Leander waved a hand. "Not as our publicist. But just—" Leander waved a hand. "You know. For an occasional night in."

What? My gut reacted at his words even though I barely knew him. "Absolutely not," I sputtered. "You aren't prostitutes! You don't have to give in to her demands."

Leander arched an eyebrow, but my mouth was still running away with me.

"We do not give in to terrorists," I continued passionately, even though no one was exactly arguing with me. Crap. *Get back on track, Hope. Get back on track.* I strove for focus. Difficult with Leander's and Janus's twin gazes piercing into me.

"So what's her most nuclear option here?" I asked rhetorically, trying to get back into game mode. "She goes to the press with a video? Deep fakes are so common these days. TikTokers do it all the time, and let me tell you, they look convincing." My eyes flashed as I looked back and forth from Janus to Leander.

I was just passionate about helping them, that was all. I hated revenge porn. I'd been terribly vigilant about protecting Makayla and Destiny from it. It was just as despicable when it was a woman doing it to a man.

Everyone had a right to privacy. That was all. Yep. Uh huh. Nothing at all to do with the twin pair of bullet-gray eyes that felt like they were piercing right through my skin.

Time to wrap up.

"She's the one who's forced you into this position," I finished emphatically. "I say you deny, deny, deny. You're hunky twins, I'm sure people have had this—"

Dammit, my cheeks flamed yet again and I dropped my

eyes but finished strong in spite of a minor stutter. "This *f-f-fantasy* about the two of you before. If she releases it, we'll put out a statement saying she's a bitter ex-employee who you had very good reason—documented good reason—to fire, and she's just viciously retaliating."

I stood up, pacing if only to get away from Janus's proximity as I finished the rest of my thought. "We inform her that if she goes forward with this revenge porn, we can go just as nuclear. We'll destroy her. And it won't be mutually assured destruction. She's the only one who will never be able to find a job again."

I looked back at Leander, eyes blazing. "You're Leander freaking Mavros. You'll come off scot-free. But if she ever wants to work again, she better keep her mouth, and her video, to herself. And if she does, then you'll provide a lovely severance package and do her the privilege of forgetting she ever existed."

Milo was nodding, obviously excited about what I was saying. "Of course. Genius."

"Plus," I said, looking around at all of them, "if it does come out, having me as your publicist will be even more protection. Which is exactly why you called me, isn't it?"

I zeroed in on Milo now, getting exactly why he'd come to me of all people. Because we really were only acquaintances. He knew lots of publicists. But he'd called *me*.

Sheepishly, Milo nodded. "No one helps us look squeakier clean than you, babe. You're known industry-wide for keeping your little Disney starlets purer than the driven snow."

Well. It only made sense. Everyone in this town used everybody else, who used them right back. That was fine. It was the way the game was played.

After all, once I'd been a publicist for Leander Mavros for a year—that was all I was willing to commit to this for—my reputation would be irrefutably established as more than just an excellent publicist for child stars. I'd officially be one of the biggest names in town, and I'd finally be able to accomplish my dream of starting my own PR firm.

One day soon, I was going to take this town by storm.

I glanced back, only to find two sets of stormy gray eyes burning my way, and an icy hot shiver ran down my spine.

If I survived the day, that was.

4

GIRL TIME ON PREMIERE NIGHT

"Oh my God, you're *where*?" Makayla screeched in my face over the phone screen.

"Shhh," I hushed her, waving a hand and walking behind a large ornate column for a little bit of privacy. People were starting to arrive at the theater—the Village Theater, that is—so most of the hubbub was outside and in the large first foyer.

I whispered as I headed down the stairs into a more shadowed and deserted area. "The Village Theater," I said to Makayla. She knew it was one of the three theaters around town where big movie premieres happened.

"For the *Trapdoor* premiere? Jesus, by the time I asked, not even my agent could get me tickets to that!"

I grinned, feeling a little thrill at being able to tell her, "It might have a little something to do with the fact that I now rep Leander Mavros."

"What?" she shrieked, even louder than she had earlier. "Shut your frippin' mouth! Oh my God, oh my God. You got the Mavros twins? Holy shit!"

I hurriedly turned down the volume on my phone because

I was starting to get strange looks from the few people milling around down here. "Jesus, Makayla, calm down. Leander Mavros isn't *that* big a deal."

"Not a big deal," she continued squealing, jumping up and down so that I had to look away from the bouncing video. But I could still *hear* her just fine: "Um, am I speaking to the same woman who forced me to watch seasons five through eight of *Who's Counting Now?* on repeat and the extended version DVDs of the twins in the one movie they did together before Janus imploded and quit acting?"

"What's that?" I said, making a crackling noise with my mouth. "Uh oh, hon, I think my signal's acting up. I'm losing you."

"Shut up, wench, I taught you that trick. Now answer the question."

I sighed and looked at her through the screen. "We watched all that as a cautionary tale for you. I didn't want your career to end up the same way as Janus's. And look at you now. Our newest superhero extraordinaire."

"Don't try to change the subject on me. I know all your tricks. Spill."

"Fine." I glanced at my phone, checking the time. I still had about ten minutes. Milo had given me a security tracking app for the limo so I could see when they were arriving.

I breathed out and leaned back against a wall. After a quick check that no one was close, I whispered the truth, "Of course I'm freaked out. I totally crushed on these guys as a teenager. But I've been around celebrities enough now. They just want to be treated like normal people. Isn't that what you've always wanted?"

Makayla pursed her lips, frowning. "Well, I mean, yeah." Then she grinned. "Except when I want to be treated like a queen. But it doesn't mean I don't still get star-struck."

I laughed at that, double checking over my shoulder our conversation was still private, but no one was lurking. Paranoia was my middle name. Had to be, in this game. "You? By whom?"

She rattled off the name of one of the biggest movie stars. Even my eyes were popping. "And? What was it like when you met him?"

She let out a disgusted noise. "He was a total dick. Tried to grab my ass within three seconds of meeting me. It's true what they say. Never meet your heroes."

I bit my lip, inadvertently thinking of Leander or Janus grabbing my ass. I straightened up immediately. Good Lord, I could *not* be thinking that kind of thing about my new bosses!

Well, I mean, they weren't exactly my bosses. They were clients. Or co-workers. Something like that... And Lord knew I'd seen what could happen between co-workers on set. Half my job with Makayla and Destiny had been keeping them protected from shenanigans on-set and on-tour.

Sure, they had boyfriends here and there, but I kept away any potentially predatory producers, agents, or promoters who gave me bad vibes. Nobody was gonna take advantage of my girls on my watch, that was for damn sure.

I might look like sugar and spice, but I had a spine of steel —and anyone who'd ever crossed me or my clients knew it.

"But I'm sure Leander and Janus aren't assholes," Makayla continued.

I shrugged. "I guess I'll find out soon enough."

"But surely you've met them already? What were they like?"

"It was a very brief meeting, when I got the job last week. Since then I've just been working with their manager. It's all been a rush since we leave on the press tour tomorrow."

"Ooo, a press tour? That sounds interesting. How long is it?"

"Three weeks."

There was a pause, and Makayla had her scheming face on. "What if they really aren't assholes? Or even if they are. So what? Maybe that's the perfect way to get rid of your V-card. Fuck a Mavros twin and get it out of your system."

My mouth dropped open. I looked over my shoulders again, then hissed back at the camera. "I cannot believe *you* of all people are saying this! Screw a celebrity just because they're a celebrity?"

She rolled her eyes. "It's different with guys."

"That's totally sexist."

Makayla lifted the phone closer to her face and rolled her eyes harder. "Look, we can be all politically correct when we're in front of cameras. But in my experience with men—"

"Since when did you go out and get all experienced? You're *nineteen*!"

"Yeah? That's legal. Plus, you were the one who got the condoms for me and Johnny. What did you think we were—?"

I laughed out loud then whispered, "Johnny Jackson does not count as a *man*. And you told me you were having sex. What else was I supposed to do?"

"Well, I've done plenty of exploring since Johnny. I know you're Hope Robins, practically perfect in every single way, and look, if you're Ace or still exploring your sexuality, that's totally cool, I don't mean to pressure you—"

"It's not that." I shook my head.

"'Cause it's totally cool. The LGBTQ community is super welcoming. I've got a bunch of friends who are—"

"Jesus, Mak, I still *fantasize*." I felt my cheeks blush bright and hot. "And, um, I'm pretty sure about my, orientation or whatever. I like guys."

Makayla watched me with that penetrating gaze of hers before shrugging. "Okay, okay, I'll back off. I'm just saying, it wouldn't kill ya to loosen up a little. Especially now that you aren't looking after kids and teenagers anymore. Leander's a big boy who can look after himself. You gotta enjoy the glitz and glamour, babe! There's more to life than work. Isn't that what you were always telling me?"

"Yeah, 'cause the afterparties are so my thing," I mocked sarcastically. "Come on, Mak, you know I can barely stand up in heels. That's why I always loved the Nickelodeon premieres where I could wear my Doc Martin's."

"Oh God, tell me you aren't packing those things on this trip."

"No comment."

"God save us all," Makayla moaned into her camera, making me laugh again. "Now, go find a mirror so I can see what you're wearing, because God as my witness, if you're pulling that shit where you're wearing a dress from Target again, I will send my entire design team to Cinderella your ass for your next press event."

"No, no, I learned my lesson," I said. "It's a lovely black Christian Siriano."

"Black?" she asked, sounding disappointed.

"Yes, so I blend in with the background, exactly as a publicist ought to."

Makayla sighed. "Are there even any sequins on it?"

I made a gagging noise. "I don't do sequins."

"How are you going to get laid without sequins?" Makayla wailed until I turned the sound down to one bar on my phone.

I didn't tell her that, on an extremely dumb impulse I already regretted, I *had* tossed a box of condoms into my duffel. The box—one of many—hadn't been meant for me; I'd bought it for Destiny when I'd been on tour with her last summer.

I wouldn't need it. It was only a three-week long publicity tour anyway.

How much trouble could I get myself into in three weeks anyway?

Just then, an alert popped up on my phone.

And I almost dropped the damn thing.

"Shit!"

"Oh my God, did you just cuss? I've never heard you cuss in ten years of knowing you."

"S-sorry, Mak, I g-g-g-gotta go. Love you, talk later."

"Hope, why are you stuttering? What's going on—"

But I just waved and then hit the red button.

Because looking down at my phone, I saw that even though she'd sounded pleasant enough when I'd called two days earlier to set up a meeting for next week—solidly *after* Leander's premiere—

My eyes tried to deny the headline they were reading splashed all over one of the top celebrity gossip sites: *Breaking News! Mavros Twins Sextape!*

Shit.

Their former publicist had gone nuclear after all, on the night of Leander's big premiere, no less.

Right as he faced the gauntlet of the red carpet.

5

$HIT HITS THE FAN

Immediately I dialed Leander's number, but it went straight to voicemail. Shaking my head, I dialed Milo instead. It rang, at least.

"Pick up, pick up," I hissed into the phone, but it just went to voicemail. "Shit!" I stared down at my phone as notification after notification popped up. I clicked on another one and then wished I hadn't.

I only saw a tangle of bodies before I immediately shut the window, stabbing repeatedly with my finger before actually managing it.

Dialing the last number I had, I hit Janus's number as I ran back up the stairs, glad I'd gone for my casual flats instead of heels, no matter what Makayla might think. I checked the clock on my phone.

Jesus. They should be arriving any minute. What the hell was I going to do? What if they didn't see the news ahead of time and weren't prepared? Now that I thought about it, I remembered Milo mentioning something about a ritual of going phone dark before premieres so Leander could get *in the right head space*.

I wondered if Geena knew that too and had timed it this way intentionally. Knowing Leander would be walking into this blind. What a bitch.

Well, it was my job to fix what other people broke, and I couldn't be precious about it. So I girded my loins and fought through the people clustered in the foyer.

"Sorry, excuse me, I need to get through." And, "I'm so sorry, pardon me." That to a big tall guy after I'd elbowed him in the side when he wouldn't move. One way or another, I made the sea part for me, until I was to the door itself.

Lena Clark, Leander's beautiful costar, was perched in the doorway, chatting and giggling with an entourage of friends.

"Hi, excuse me, coming through," I called as I barreled towards them.

Lena only glanced my way, then laughed to her friends and stayed put.

"Pardon me," I said, louder as I got closer.

Lena turned her skewering gaze on me. "What the hell do you think you're doing out here? The waitstaff is supposed to stay in the back."

Waitstaff? This dress was designer! Just wait till I told Makayla. See, no one could tell the difference between a designer dress and Target after all. A little black dress was a little black dress.

I gave her a flat smile. "I'll tell them if I see them. Now please move aside."

Her eyebrows went up tartly but one of her friends tugged her to the side. "Just move aside, Len? Can we not get into a catfight for one night?"

I didn't have time for this. I lightly pushed Lena to the side, just enough so I could get past her.

She made a shocked, offended noise but I couldn't care. I was on a mission to warn the twins.

I heard her and her friend chattering, probably about me and my rudeness, and rolled my eyes. But it was literally my *job* to protect Leander, and Janus too for that matter, because they were kind of a package deal. A Janus scandal would just be as bad as Leander, and the fact that this involved *both* of them...

The air of the cool night hit me like a shock after the stuffy insides of the theater, along with the noise of the roaring crowd, but I didn't let it slow me down.

The red carpet was long, lined with photographers, videographers, and journalists of every stripe. Beyond them were fans crowded around, all hoping for a glimpse of their favorite celebrity. It was an amazing turnout. Calm theater attendants helped usher along the less notable attendees while encouraging celebrities to linger, a hundred microphones shoved in their face as more and more limos lined up down the block.

But as I looked down at my app, I saw Milo was pulling up next.

Crap, how was I going to get to them in time?

Without being able to call them, the only way to communicate with them was, well, the old-fashioned way.

So I ignored the attendant who called, "Ma'am, where are you going? You can't go backwards down the carpet!" and headed down the steps, dodging a woman in a gorgeous hoop ballgown and making a sprint for it.

"Hey!" someone called behind me. "Stop her!"

I held up my press badge over my shoulder. "I'm allowed to be here," I called, my eyes zeroed in on Leander's limo.

They were pulling up to the carpet and I saw half the gathered folks pulling out their phones and checking them—no doubt because they also had the same celebrity news notifications lighting up their screens.

I used the moment of distraction to shove another theater

attendant aside just as he'd opened the door to the limo and Leander peeked a head out, about to step out into the chaos.

A frown registered on his handsome, chiseled features as I all but barreled into him, pushing him back into the limo. The sides of our bodies were pressed together and for a second all I could feel was lean, muscular male. And his hand still firmly on my upper arm where he'd caught me right before we collided, the attendant still chasing after me.

"I'm *so* sorry, Mr. Mavros!" He came huffing after us, stopping me from shutting the door. "I'll call security immediately."

"Don't be foolish," Leander bit out. "This is my publicist."

His eyes raked me up and down, and I realized that in my dash-and-crash, the skirt of my dress had hiked scandalously up my more-than-ample thighs.

"Why didn't you say so?" the attendant asked me accusingly, but I just shook my head and looked back at Leander. We didn't have time for any of this, not even the blush blasting my cheeks as I dragged my dress back down.

"Is your phone on? Have any of you seen what's happening?"

Leander shook his head and Janus went on alert from the couch across from where Leander was sitting. "What's up?"

Leander glared at the attendant until he backed away and we were able to close the door.

It was so suddenly silent after the roaring crowd that it took me a second to gather my bearings, but just a second.

"She did it. Geena leaked the story."

Leander shot upright, his body pulling all the way away from mine for the first time since we'd gotten in the limo. I felt foolish even for noticing.

"She did not."

But I nodded vigorously. They needed to catch up to current events, like *yesterday*.

"She did. And the second you step out that door, you're going to get a thousand questions about it. We have about three seconds to come up with an action plan. Which I did already. And it's, 'No Comment. No comment, no comment, no comment.'"

I looked from one man to the other. "Got it? We all on the same page?"

"I'm at a movie premiere for the movie I fucking star in," Leander said, eyes flashing. "I can't just say 'no comment' about a scandal I'm directly implicated in."

"Did she leak the footage or just the story?" Janus asked. "How bad is it?"

"Everything," I said flatly.

Believe me, I remembered all too well the brief flash of entangled bodies I'd glimpsed. A manly ass thrusting from behind while another man held her on his lap from underneath. The video was good enough quality that you could make out the expression of concentrated pleasure on the twin facing the camera. That alone had been almost hotter than the rest of it.

I averted my eyes and hope they couldn't read the thoughts all over my face. "It's out there. All of it. The video already has three million hits. It's gone viral."

"*Fuck*." This from Janus.

I took a deep breath. "Look, in the morning we'll do the deep dive response about how easy deep fakes are and the whole spiel. Tonight you just need to say you're as shocked as everyone else. And say 'no comment.'" I winced. "They'll try to go for the jugular to get a reaction out of you. To get the scoop for their outlet."

I looked at Leander, dead serious. "Do. Not. Bite. I repeat, do *not* take the bait."

Unlike me, it was clear that Leander's cheeks did not get red when he was frustrated. No, he just went paler and paler. I didn't realize it at first, but this was what Leander looked like when he was truly pissed off. Janus got it, though, because he immediately put a hand out on his brother's arm.

"You're out, baby brother," Janus said.

Leander jerked away from his brother's grip, his eyes immediately shooting to me.

Milo nodded but Leander's gaze jerked away from me, and from the murderous look on his face, it seemed like he wanted to punch the both of them.

I just looked back and forth between them all, confused.

"Enjoy my fucking movie," Leander said, throwing a metal cocktail shaker across the limo, where it banged silently to the carpeted floor. I jumped in surprise, but he didn't apologize. He glared out the window, the only giveaway the fury in his eyes and his flaring nostrils as he grabbed for his tie, yanking it loose.

Wait, what was happening?

But Janus cleared it up by taking my arm. "I've got this one," he said.

Leander looked back our way, glaring at Janus's hand on my arm.

Then, as an attendant knocked on the window, yelling that there were cars getting backed up behind us, Janus opened the door. He held out a hand to me and then I was being pulled along the seat and out behind him.

I only got one last glimpse of a still furious looking Leander as the door closed and then the limo drove off.

Again, the cacophony of the crowd hit like a surge. But

beside me, Janus looked calm as ever, standing straight. He strode down the red carpet as if he did this all the time.

And suddenly I wondered… did he? Just how often did the two brothers switch places? In identical tuxes, it was nigh impossible to tell one from the other.

Then there was no time for puzzling it out any further because Janus had stepped up and started fielding questions.

Reporters shouted all kinds of things at him with microphones held out for his response:

"Do you like having sex with your brother?"

"Leander! Leander! How do you respond to the charges of sexual harassment in the workplace?"

"Leander! Where's Janus? Don't you do *everything* together?" Snickers from the crowd before more shouting came.

My face flamed even though I knew I had to stay back. My place was in the shadows even though I wanted to shield my client from every bit of this. Their former publicist had made sure that would be impossible, though. She'd exposed them in every way possible. Why on earth had they ever gotten involved with a woman like that?

And what was Leander thinking now? Was he in that limo reading everything that had been written about the two of them? Tossing around more cocktail-ware? I felt just as furious, but I could do more than throw things. Dammit, I needed to be on a laptop somewhere doing damage control right now.

But supporting Leander… well, *Janus*, I guessed, right now, as he faced down these vultures, was the most important thing. So I stood tall in the background, out of the way of pictures, while more questions were flung like arrows Janus's way.

"Aren't you canceled now? Why did you even show up tonight?"

Followed by an even more vulgar question.

I winced. Jesus, they weren't holding back, were they?

But Janus just held out his arms to quiet the questions coming at him. Cameras were flashing so nonstop I knew he'd be so blind he wouldn't be able to even see the first twenty minutes of the movie, that was, if he ever got inside.

But movie premieres were never about watching the movie, not really, were they? They were all about this. The drama out front. Who wore what. Who let what scandalous tidbit slip with a reporter.

Everyone here was hungry for a show.

Then Janus snatched one of the mikes being held out towards him. What the hell was he doing? I tried to wave and get his attention.

No comment, I mouthed at him. But he wasn't looking at me. Nope, he just confidently walked back to the center of the carpet, looking for all the world like a showman in complete control of the circus around him.

I paused, watching him, and so did most everyone else.

The cacophony of voices even quieted some. At the realization that something different was happening, that they were witnessing a *moment*, the camera flashes went even crazier. A hundred cell phones lifted to capture what he would say next.

Oh crap, I'd told him to say *no comment*, and unless he was hushing the crowd to give one big, anti-climactic, "no comment," I was about to have a helluva lot more to do tomorrow than I'd expected.

Because I had no freaking idea what was about to come out of Janus Mavros's mouth. And that was always a PR agent's worst nightmare.

"Quiet if you want to hear me make a statement about the troublesome, disgusting news I've only just heard," Janus shouted into the mike. It had the intended effect.

The crowd quieted as if a god had commanded it.

Because one had.

It wasn't so quiet one could hear a pin drop—no, there was still an underground current of murmuring. But too many people were hoping for a good sound bite. These were professionals, and they quieted one another harshly, doing his work for him.

"I'll have a clearer statement in the morning," Janus said. "But frankly, my brother Janus and I were shocked. So shocked Janus couldn't even get out of the limo just now. To have our bond so twisted, and by someone we *trusted*." Janus contorted his handsome face.

"So you're denying the allegations? The *video*?" someone called.

Janus laughed in their face. "The video? People make deep fakes of us all the time. I only heard of this five minutes ago but look what someone sent me yesterday! Before any of this."

He reached in his pocket and I waited with bated breath along with everyone else as he pulled out his phone. He clicked on something, then faced the phone outwards. I struggled against some of the other press to try to see what was on the screen.

"I don't know if you can see that," he spoke into the mike. "But a fan made a deepfake of me playing Loki in the next Marvel movie." He named the fan page so everyone could check it out for themselves.

Everyone started clicking away on their own phones, and since I couldn't see Janus's, so did I. And soon I along with everyone else at the premiere had clicked on a video on a fan TikTok page which had an obviously deep-faked video of Leander. The tinny sound played in echoes all over the dais.

And all of a sudden I went from anxious to giddy. Because it was a good fake. It was obvious only in that it was from a movie with a well-known actor but had Leander's face instead —otherwise, the image was very smooth.

Murmurs started through the crowd and I felt my eyebrows go up, impressed in spite of myself. While I knew the tech was possible, I hadn't seen a ton of well-done examples of it.

Janus pulled the mike back to his mouth. "It's sad how many people will try to capitalize on celebrity. And sad how quick most people are to believe the worst. Now, I'm going to go inside and enjoy the movie I thought we were all here to celebrate. I loved making it, and I hope audiences love it just as much as I do."

And then he held out the mike to his side and dropped it.

To the roaring cheer of the mob, who just like that had gone from wanting his blood to adoring him again in five minutes flat.

6

THE AFTER PARTY

"So do they do that a lot?" I asked Milo, letting out a loud breath as I finally sat down for what felt like the first time all night.

I tapped the private bartop and asked for a vodka tonic.

Milo looked up. He'd been standing by the wall near the bar, calmly clocking the party. "What?"

There'd been a lull between songs, but another loud one started and I had to stand up and talk almost in Milo's ear so he could hear my answer. "Switch places like that."

Milo just smiled mildly as he pulled back from me and shook his head. It was dimly lit in this mansion in the Hollywood Hills, and the interior design had the inspiration of a nineties coke den. The stool I was sitting on was the only comfy seat in the joint. Everything, including the furniture, was all pointy edges.

There were about a jillion lights embedded in the ceiling everywhere, but they were all turned dramatically low. Then a strobe light went on at the same time a low bass beat dropped. It had the intended effect of drawing people back on the "dance floor."

They spared no expense for parties like this. The most elite of the Hollywood elite were here. Stars in their natural habitat.

I had already counted three Oscar winners and countless Emmy winners among the bunch. Even one EGOT superstar.

Not that I was one to be starstruck.

I shook my head in disbelief as I held a champagne flute loosely in my hand. It was the first time I'd slowed down all night. I'd missed the entire movie, fielding calls and handling press. I'd used Janus's spontaneous statement as a jumping off point, leading everyone to the deepfake on the fan account he'd mentioned and pointing out how easy the technology was these days.

Then I started drafting a statement for tomorrow, short and sweet, that I'd have both twins look over before I sent it off in the morning. Well, I'd done that in between fielding calls, and by the end of them I didn't even have to manufacture my outrage at the questions I was getting. I found revenge porn disgusting on every level and I would lie, beg, borrow, or cheat, if I could help them out of it.

"I think it'll blow over," Milo said.

I looked up in surprise at Milo just as the bartender returned with my drink. The music had chilled out to a low dance zombie beat that I just bet went great with whatever party drug was currently circulating right now. But it did make it easier to talk. "The scandal?"

He grinned at me, showing off his big, straight white teeth. "What scandal?" He held out his arms gregariously. "Tomorrow it'll be gone. Because of you."

I laughed and swiped at my mouth with my napkin. "If it does, it'll be because of him." I gestured with my glass towards Janus.

But Milo just shook his head. "What, that? He got that

deep fake idea from you. He went looking for it after you mentioned it at the meeting the other day, just to have on hand if anything like this happened. Fuck, none of us thought we'd need it sooner rather than later."

He shook his head, then went back to watching the party.

"So are you on duty right now?"

He bobbled his head back and forth. "I have my security guys downstairs and at the doors, but I always like to keep an eye on things when we're out like this."

When he said, "like this," did he mean when Janus was acting as Leander? I hadn't missed that Milo never answered my initial question.

My eyes strayed back to Janus, sitting in the circle of pointy couches across the open space from us. People were crowded all around him—including some very famous faces, such as Leander's costar I'd had the *lovely* run-in with earlier, Lena. Did they know it was Janus, or did they all believe he was Leander?

Lena certainly wasn't paying him any mind. The entourage that had come with her, though? Women were gathered on either side of Janus. A few had somehow become magically more unclad as the night drew on. Janus didn't seem to mind their attention. He certainly wasn't pushing them away.

Did he enjoy pretending to be his brother and coming out for all the love and adulation of being a celebrity? It was such a different picture than had been painted of him by the media. Either he was just as good an actor as his brother or... they'd had some excellent freaking PR somewhere along the way.

A leggy blonde pretended to knock over her drink and half-fall into his lap while she "cleaned" it up.

I turned away and rolled my eyes. Then remembered how I'd barreled into Leander earlier and ended up all but in *his* lap. Feeling my cheeks flame, I took another swig of my drink and turned back to Milo. "So what about you? Where do you fit in all this?"

Milo frowned. "I'm the manager, but you know that. I guess I haven't explained the security thing. I'm the head of security, but that's mainly just a title. Mostly I schedule and run the guys from a couple different agencies we use."

I tilted my head at him. "Yeah. Duh. But I'm trying to get a feel for this place. For you guys. The dynamics of it all. People think that working PR is about spin, but they're wrong. When people call me a *fixer*, yeah, they're right. But it's not just because I come in and fix the public perception of things. I like to dig in and find out what's really going on. To fix *people*."

Milo laughed. "Well, after today I'd think you've gotten a pretty good picture of what's going on here. We're a fucking mess." He grinned that big full-toothed grin at me again. "Think you can fix us?"

"Oh no," I laughed. "That came out all wrong. I mean, I would never try. I don't try to *fix* people, fix people, like I think they're broken, just like a *fixer*, the term, you know." I threw my hands in the air. "I'm gonna stop talking now. I'm no one to judge anyway, I'm far from perfect." I swigged down the last of my drink.

Milo laughed out loud. "Nope. Don't believe it. If anyone's perfect, you're it."

"Ugh, *no*, God," I slammed down my glass on the bar, feeling a pleasant buzz. "Please. Anything but perfect. I'm so *tired* of being Miss Virginal Perfect all the time!"

Milo had just taken a sip of Coke and he all but spit it all out. Right all over my Christian Siriano LBD.

"Virginal?" he coughed. Then he was grabbing a napkin off the bar and reaching for my cleavage before yanking back right at the last moment. "Shit, sorry—"

I grabbed his arm in a vise grip. "Oh my god, I can't believe I told you that. Swear you won't tell anyone. *Swear.*"

I shook him until he made a noise I took to be assent. Then he looked around, his eyes wide, especially when he zeroed in on a corner not far from us. What? I looked around too.

A little further away, someone had started doing body shots off a naked girl and in a dark corner, one man had dropped to his knees to suck off another guy.

My stomach did a deep *swish* and I jerked my eyes away.

"Come on," Milo said, putting an arm around my shoulders. "You shouldn't be here."

I pulled away, laughing. "Are you kidding? Just because some people are getting frisky in the corner? I'm twenty-seven."

"You say that like it means something. You're still a child."

I was pissed. Jesus, all this because I let slip that I was a virgin?

"What's going on here, you crazy kids?" came a cool, deep voice that immediately had chills running up my spine.

Janus had somehow snuck up behind me.

I held a hand to my chest, still a bit damp from Milo's spit take at my idiotic spontaneous confession. "You scared me," I said, once I finally found my voice again.

He just glanced coolly down at my chest, his life of the party persona disappearing in an instant. "You're all wet. You two looked like you were in some sort of heated discussion. I got curious."

Was I crazy or did the eyes he flashed at Milo say *jealous* instead of curious? Okay, now I *knew* that was the vodka talking. Because that was crazy. He'd just been surrounded by a ton of models fawning all over him.

And I was... I was...

Too drunk to be taking any more of this day in.

"I think I'm gonna go catch an Uber home," I said, forcing a bright smile for the both of them. "Tomorrow, we leave for New York and if we thought today was a long day, well—" I held my hands out, hoping for a quick exit.

But Janus startled me by saying, "We've already had your things brought to the mansion. It was good you'd already packed."

I froze out of shock. He'd— They'd, *what*—

"We got notice from security that there are paparazzi outside the gates here. I didn't want anyone following you home and learning your address."

His eyes smoldered at me. "So you're coming home with us."

7

AFTER THE AFTER PARTY

I couldn't sleep that night. I mean, how the hell was I supposed to sleep after the night I'd just had? And look where I was now!

Everywhere I looked, everything was the finest quality. Silk sheets. Carpet my toes were currently luxuriating in. A private bathroom suite with rain shower heads. I'd spent almost forty-five minutes in there luxuriating in the steam and had just gotten out. I was currently wrapped in the fluffiest down robe. I felt like I'd checked into a spa.

It was still taking all of my professional maturity not to send a girlish text to Makayla squeeing over the fact that I was actually sleeping under the same roof as the Mavros twins. In a guest bedroom. But still!

I hadn't meant to be here tonight.

But then nothing had gone as plan today, had it?

They hadn't been kidding about the paparazzi. They chased us down the highway on all sides, blinding flashes occasionally lighting up the night as they tried to get pictures through the thick black windows of the SUV. At least the highways were mostly empty at two in the morning—the only time of day that could be said of traffic in LA.

On the way home, Milo had ordered me to sit up front with him, and when we finally got to the gated mansion the twins shared, Janus was snoring. Milo woke him and he stumbled into the house.

Milo then bustled me upstairs right after we parked. The house had been mostly dark so I'd barely gotten a look around at the sumptuous mansion. And that was fine. I was here to do a job, not gawk. Tomorrow would be here soon enough and the three-week press tour we had scheduled would be grueling. Which was why I really should be going to bed.

Instead, I kept pacing, digging my toes into the carpet. Because in spite of feeling tired earlier after the premiere, now I felt supremely *wired.*

Last night had been my first real after-party—one where I wasn't there playing mother hen or picking up the pieces when my charge was barfing up their lungs in a bathroom somewhere. And I hadn't even been able to enjoy it like I thought I might.

Those just weren't my people. I didn't think going to a party like that could ever be anything more than a sociology project for a girl like me. I watched like a wallflower, studying all the beautiful people in their natural habitat. I was a celebrity hanger-on, and I knew they didn't really want my kind mixing and mingling.

I'd always been happy with that before. Just watching. The thrill of getting to be in the room where it was all happening had been enough for me. I'd always focused on rubbing elbows with the power players in the industry and earning respect from those that mattered.

That had been all I cared about.

Before.

So why did I light up every time Janus brushed against me? Because several times tonight he *had* gone out of his way to touch me.

No, I shook my head. It was only my mind playing tricks on me. Probably because I'd just spent hours with reporters talking through very explicit details about the things he and his brother had done in that tape. Dear Lord, a woman should never know details like that about her very attractive clients!

I shook the ridiculous thoughts away. Regardless of Makayla's fantasies, I was a professional first and foremost. Any lingering teenage crushes would not get in the way of me doing my job.

Plus, I was sure I'd find things not to like about the twins that would turn me off from any silly girlish crushes soon.

For instance, I'd been sure Janus would either stay behind or invite one of those gorgeous women he'd been chatting up all night back home with us. He'd stayed in their company all night; I'd been sure he would go home with one of them.

But then he'd left them there with barely a backwards glance. Or maybe that was how he always was with women.

Walking over to the window that looked out onto darkness, I knew I should climb in bed and try to sleep.

I *was* exhausted. Physically. I'd regret the lack of sleep tomorrow.

But I still felt like bouncing off the walls. None of my other gigs had felt like this. Yes, I always found starting with a new client exciting. I loved that my work was so project based and that no day was ever the same twice.

This was different, though.

This was like... I don't know, like there was this energy, or anticipation, for what was about to happen.

It was ridiculous and hyperbolic to even think it, but it felt like something big was about to happen. And for once, not just to my client.

It felt like I was on the Titanic and there were icebergs in the water. There was danger all around.

And I still wanted to go full steam ahead.

A smarter woman would slow down and ask herself what the hell she was doing.

But God, I was so tired of being the smart one.

So instead of doing what I usually did when I had restless energy in the middle of the night and rereading Jane Eyre for the ninety-seventh time until I fell asleep, I got up instead.

No one else was awake, I was sure. The huge house was silent except for a mechanical hum that might be a refrigerator or the air conditioner or some other fancy appliance I'd never heard of. Everything in this house was *smart*, apparently. Milo had quickly tried to explain some of it when we'd come in, but I'd been busy not getting lost as he led me to where I'd be staying.

But I *had* noted where the kitchen was. It was a habit of regularly living a life of travel—always know where the food was. In all the craziness of the day and night, I'd barely gotten a few mouthfuls of food and I was starving. I'd been hoping to just sleep it off but now my stomach was grumbling too loudly to ignore.

I padded down the large central staircase in my socks and had just opened the fridge when—

"That was crazy tonight, huh?"

I about jumped out of my skin as I spun around to see Janus standing right behind me.

"Jesus!" I gasped.

I'd thought I was totally alone but he must have already been in the darkened kitchen to have snuck up on me so suddenly. Or, well, I guess technically I'd snuck up on him if he'd been here first.

"Not quite," he said with a sardonic smirk. "Sorry to startle you."

In the light of the still-open fridge I could see a slight smile on his face. "Old habits die hard. My brother and I are always sneaking up and trying to scare the shit out of each other."

I laughed and put a hand to my chest. "Well, consider me scared."

His smile grew, I think because I hadn't taken offense. He leaned against the counter as if he'd decided he was staying awhile. "So? What'd you think of the afterparty?"

I shrugged, wondering what my hair looked like. I'd just thrown it up in a bun after scrubbing all of tonight's makeup off my face. "I don't know. It's not really for me, is it? Did you have fun?"

He frowned, looking confused. "Why isn't it for you? Those things are for people in the industry. You're in the industry."

I laughed out loud at that, feeling immediately at ease and relaxing. "They're for celebrities and people hoping to either see celebrities or be seen with celebrities."

"And that's not you?" He quirked an eyebrow up.

I rolled my eyes. "Let's just say I know my place. I play the game and get to know who I need to know. Which is usually the other folks in the shadows with me."

He tilted his head, like he was appraising me. "Some PR reps play the game by hobnobbing with the big names. They become influencers themselves."

I smirked at that. "Not the good ones."

And then I looked around for the clock and saw the time on the oven. "So what are you doing up at 3:28 in the morning? Because you *were* partying hard. And" —I bit my lip wondering if

I should say more but daring since he'd opened the conversation — "you were so quiet on the way home." I shrugged, hurrying to follow up, "I figured that you liked to just decompress in your own way after these things. So many people out there want a piece of you. Even if you are just playing the part of your brother."

Janus smirked, but the look was darker than anything I'd seen from him all evening. "Yeah, well, Leander can be a temperamental little shit sometimes." He looked like he wanted to say more but then stopped himself.

He took a step closer, leaning an arm up above me, capturing me against the open fridge. Cold at my back, him warm at my front. I shivered.

It was absurd, but I wanted to reach up a hand to his face. He was cold too, in spite of his hot body. I could see it there. A coldness deep inside him, shining through his icy gaze. A coldness and an emptiness that hadn't been there earlier in the night.

I gasped, and when I did, my chest rose—including my breasts. The small movement pressed my chest into his.

But I couldn't even care about it because what I was so shocked by what I'd just realized.

"You aren't Janus," I whispered. "*You're* Leander."

He looked surprised but smiled with pleasure.

"Now that, Ms. Robins, is a talent. Only our birth mother could tell us apart. Our adoptive parents were constantly getting us confused. The world too."

I blinked, the whole evening coming into focus. I put the same question to him I had put to Milo earlier. "How often do y'all do this? Switch?"

He opened his eyes, the picture of innocence. "I have no idea what you're talking about. And if you value your NDA, neither do you."

I rolled my eyes. "I'm a locked box when it comes to secrets. Not only is it part of my job but it's just..." I shrugged. "It's always been my way. All my friends knew I was the one to come talk to when they needed to spill and it would never get out."

Leander arched an eyebrow, and was it just my imagination, or had he leaned in even further? My breath came shorter as he spoke. "I know nothing on your clients has ever hit the press. And we dug. But maybe they just happened to live like little angels."

His proximity was making me giddy so my laugh might have been a little shrill. "Excellent. Then I did my job well. Because they were teenage girls who made mistakes like everyone else. They shouldn't have been expected to be angels. That's a bullshit standard our society holds young women to."

His curious look returned. "But nothing ever broke about them."

"Just because society *shouldn't* be made of mobs of internet trolls doesn't mean it isn't. And while they were freaking *children*, minors who weren't even of age. Hell yeah, I protected them using every trick I had in the book." My words were coming out passionately by the end because this was a subject I was passionate about.

Too many in this industry were happy to use up young talent with no concern for the mental health of the kids involved. They had people trying to use them from every angle while they were a viable income source—ad agencies, TV networks, their agents, their families, everyone else in the industry who peripherally relied on them for jobs, down to the audio producers and craft services.

It was an insane amount of pressure and I was surprised

more young stars didn't flame out by their twenties considering some of the stuff I'd seen go on around my girls.

"So what you're saying is, you can keep a secret," he said, leaning in even further, and considering our chests were already so close—

I gasped again, but this time because I realized his face was leaning close to mine. And I—

I was so stupid I actually thought he was going to kiss me.

When he didn't, and his head kept moving, I was mortified. Oh Jesus Christ, was he just reaching for something in the fridge, and I thought he'd been about to *kiss* me of all things!

But then those selfsame lips made contact—with my neck.

I shuddered at the touch.

Holy shit, his lips were soft.

"Is this okay?" he asked, the gentlest whisper in the otherwise quiet night.

'Twas the night after the movie premiere and all were asleep in the house, not a creature was stirring, except for the exceptionally hot movie star necking with the horny woman who was in way over her head.

"I— Um—"

He started to pull away and in a panic, I reached up and yanked him back towards me. I was shocked at myself for the action and let go almost as soon as I'd touched him.

But when Leander chuckled, a slow, deep laugh, it had me quivering in places I couldn't even name. I'd never felt anything like—

I inhaled sharply, half of me wanting to flee back up the stairs and the other half wanting to grab his neck again and drag his lips back to my neck.

The sane part of my mind fought to the surface. Client. Leander was a client!

Leander was also Leander freaking Mavros.

So was I just another fangirl to him? An easy lay when he was feeling randy in the middle of the night?

I pulled away from his lips on my neck with a gasp.

"We shouldn't," I gulped, my better judgement finally winning out against the ridiculous pleasure rising up inside me.

Leander looked surprised, and a little perplexed as I took another short step back from him. I didn't turn and run away like I ought to have. He wasn't used to being turned down, that I could see plainly on his face.

Just another reason to turn and run. He was a player. Obviously far more sexually experienced than I was. Ha! Even if I *hadn't been* a virgin, this guy was in a whole different league.

"We shouldn't?" he asked softly. He stayed where he was and didn't approach, but his eyes seared into mine. "Why not? I can see your pulse fluttering in your throat."

When he took a small step forward and pressed his thumb against the throbbing vein at my throat... It was so absurdly pleasurable, the small touch of his cool hand against my delicate throat—

I barely kept the moan inside.

I didn't move or tell him to stop. He wrapped his other fingers lightly around my neck, applying the slightest pressure.

My mind spun as pleasure roared to life in my body. To listen to my better judgement and pull away... *or* stay and give in to his commanding touch...

8

MIDNIGHT SNACK

Holy crap.

Who was this guy? Who was I? I was a woman feeling a sexual thrill from the hottest man I'd ever shared airspace with putting his hand around my throat. He wasn't choking me. No, this was an explicitly sexual gesture.

And dear *Lord* did my body respond. I whimpered a little but was too turned on to be embarrassed by it.

"I want to touch you," he whispered in the dark.

"Okay," I whispered back, his commanding touch still around my neck.

He moved quickly. Not so quick I couldn't have stopped him, but quick enough that it took my breath away at the way my body responded when he pushed me back against the counter. He snugly fit his body between my legs, which he pushed open, hands on my knees.

He wasn't shy about pressing in against me, and the firm pressure of him there in the spot where he'd created such an ache, oh *God*—

"What are we doing?" I breathed out, some last little bit of sanity trying to scream through the rising sensations that were so foreign and overwhelming.

"Getting to know each other," Leander whispered back, his large, cool hand never wavering as it slid up my thigh from my knee all the way to the waistband of my pajama pants.

My eyes all but rolled back in my head at the strong, sensual sureness of his touch.

And then his fingers dipped inside.

"Fuck, you don't shave," he groaned, leaning his body against mine as his hand dropped lower. He twisted his wrist so that he was palming me. "I love these little curls."

Palming me... *there*.

I gasped again and slumped into him. "Leander," I hissed in shock as I reached up to clench his shoulders.

"Am I everything you fantasized about?" he asked.

I frowned, trying to catch his gaze. Was that what he thought this was? That I was just using him to live out some celebrity fantasy? But his head was bowed down, and it was clear he was watching his own hand disappear inside my pajama bottoms. Damn, that was hot.

This seemed too important a piece to simply let go, though. So in spite of the pleasure threatening to buckle my knees, I cupped his cheek. I wanted his eyes. He immediately looked up at me like he was surprised by the touch.

"I'm right here," I said, my voice tremulous with pleasure. "In this moment with you. Leander, the man."

He kept eye contact, his brows furrowing with intensity as his palm began to move against my sex.

And then I forgot about whatever point I'd been trying to prove because Jesus *God*. He was— I'd never— How could—? Oh, oh, *oh*—

I bent my face into his shoulder and my teeth sank in as he rubbed me.

And then, oh God, then he dipped his finger inside my slick wetness. And a pleasure I'd never known my body was capable of burst through me like a bright light and then rippled outwards.

I was left gasping in shock and clinging to Leander like a ragdoll.

Holy shit!

He'd just made me come. In less than three minutes, Leander Mavros had fingered me and made me come.

I mean, I had tried masturbating a few times but it never really went anywhere. I figured I either didn't understand it, wasn't doing it right, or simply wasn't built that way.

And yet here, with one touch of a gorgeous movie star god in a darkened kitchen, I was coming like a freight train. Even as the blissful feelings dissipated, I felt hungry for them all over again. It had all happened so quickly, it barely felt real.

Frankly, I wanted to climb Leander like a tree and hump him until that feeling hit again. Holy crap, if this was what sex could really be like, no wonder people talked about it all the time and wrote songs and books about it!

I mean, good *Lord.*

"You liked that, I take it?" Leander's voice was smirking and self-satisfied. Anyone else sounding like that and I would've thought they were an arrogant asshole. But no, Leander had every right to sound so smug.

"You're r-r-really good at that." Oh my God, I hadn't had a stutter since I was a kid, but he'd blown me so off-kilter that apparently it was back. I couldn't care. "R-r-really g-g-g-good." I dropped my head face-first against his chest and inhaled. "J-just need a m-minute."

"You okay there?" he asked, sounding a little concerned.

"J-j-just never done that," I confessed, face still in his shirt.

He laughed. "What, been finger-fucked in a penthouse kitchen?"

Well crap, I wasn't about to admit my virginal status now. So I laughed it off. "Something like that," I murmured, pushing from where he'd pinned me between his hot body and the cool countertop.

"You're running away again," Leander said, frown line appearing between his brows like earlier. "Why are you always doing that? I've barely begun to taste you."

And just like that, he put the finger he'd had inside me, still slick with my juices, in his mouth. He sucked it long and deep. The way his nostrils flared, you'd have thought it was the finest ambrosia.

My legs were jelly. A reckless part of me wanted to go back and wrap my legs around him. But if he'd undone me that much with the mere twitch of his fingers? We were still strangers, no matter how much I felt like I knew him.

I continued to put distance between us. With every step away from him I took, my head seemed to clear more and more.

But my body remembered all too vividly the heights he'd brought me to.

I ran my hand shakily through my hair.

"See you in the morning," I managed unevenly, clinging to what composure I could as I backed away from the fridge and the gorgeous movie star—still haloed from behind by the light of the open fridge. I realized the fridge had started to beep from being open so long, though I only now registered the noise. "Nice, um, running into you."

He smirked at me.

"Sleep tight, little Hope," he said, his voice a whisper in the shadows as I raced back up the stairs.

9

MORNING AFTER

My body was electric with what Leander had awakened in me. How had I made it through twenty-seven years of life without ever experiencing *that*?

I bounded downstairs the next morning, thrilled and slightly terrified to see if the same chemistry would still be there between me and Leander in the daylight.

But when I got to the kitchen and found Milo and one of the twins sipping coffee, I could immediately tell by his posture that it was Janus, not Leander. Don't ask me how I knew, I just did. There was something about the way the two brothers carried themselves. At least when cameras weren't rolling and paparazzi weren't around.

"Where's Leander?" I asked, and Janus looked up.

"How do you know I'm not Leander?"

I rolled my eyes and grabbed an orange from a basket in the center of the counter, peeling it while I popped some English muffins in the toaster. "You're not."

"Yeah, but how did you *know*?"

I waved a hand. "So where is he? There's not much time before we've got to go."

Milo made a face. "He heard we were flying commercial and caught a ride with Lena since she chartered a private jet. She only invited *him*, though, apparently. We're stuck in the cheap seats that got booked when Geena was barely doing her job."

But I was still fixated on *caught a ride with Lena*. Leander and Lena had dated for a while, during the movie shoot. And now, during these few weeks of doing press together, would they rekindle their romance?

All of a sudden I was furious. Why was Leander playing Handsy McHandsy with me in the kitchen last night if he was gonna just get back with his co-star the next day?

I shook my head, feeling foolish for letting my emotions run away with me like this. These guys were all players and I couldn't forget it. If I was gonna lose my V-card to one of them, I couldn't make it out to be more than it was. Just fun and games.

Still, I couldn't deny the stab of disappointment that hit me low in the stomach.

I'd live. I'd gotten through plenty of disappointments before and I'd survive this one too.

"I'll try to get y'all on private jets from now on, " I said, "but it was too late to change at the last minute. I had to work with what was already booked."

Milo and Janus really were cool about it, but while it was true that they could handle traveling commercial, it was less clear that the commercial airline could handle *them* traveling *it*.

We were swamped by paparazzi from almost the second we got to the airport. Everyone assumed Janus was Leander, naturally. The more they crowded around, the less I felt like I could breathe, even as Milo fought to keep a perimeter around Janus and me.

Eventually, airport security came and helped get us to a private VIP lounge until we got on the plane, but Janus was bothered all throughout the flight for autographs. And it only got worse once we landed in New York.

Almost as if the paps were waiting for us... like they'd known exactly when our plane would arrive. That was when it sunk in, and I should have realized it much earlier.

Geena.

"Geena must have leaked our itinerary." I shared my thoughts with Milo and he nodded, face grim after we finished fighting our way into our downtown hotel.

"I was just thinking the same. It's usually bad, but it's only this bad when she leaked our location." At my wide-eyed stare, he waved a hand. "She only did it a few times early on when Leander was trying to cinch his first Emmy nom, but he told her to knock it off. He hates crowds like this."

Yeah, my heart was still racing after the harrowing trip from our vehicle into the hotel. We'd been mobbed. Janus had put his arm around me to protect me from a bottle that had come flying our way. Not all fans were lovers.

I was still breathing heavily even though we were now safely in a conference room blocked off by hotel security. They were double checking our hotel suite was secure, considering the state of things outside.

I just shook my head. "If Geena leaked when and where we were going after the airport, she probably leaked the rest of the itinerary she booked. I need to rebook everything with new vendors or the entire trip will be like this."

"Shit," Janus said, realizing the implications. "I should've realized earlier."

When there was a roar of voices outside the door, Milo

walked several feet away and began chattering intensely over the phone with the security detail he'd arranged for New York. Was the situation escalating out there? What was happening?

"I don't think we should stay here," I said and Janus frowned and nodded, especially as the noise outside got louder.

Then the doors burst open. Janus stepped in front of me, arms out protectively. It was such a sweet, if ridiculous, gesture. He was the celebrity. I was a nobody. If a mob came through that door, it was him they'd rip to pieces, not me.

I tried to grab his arm and yank him behind some tables—a flimsy barrier but at least something—and then I saw who was leading the entourage through the door.

It was Lena Clark, followed by her entourage of sycophants.

And finally, a pale and glowering Leander stomped through the doors, slamming them behind him. Right before they shut, I glimpsed hotel security and some men dressed all in black—Milo's men, no doubt—barely holding the crowd back.

"Leander! Sign my boobs!"

"Leander! Marry me! *Leander!*"

Then the doors shut, and Leander strode towards Lena. "What the fuck?" Leander all but shouted. "Your guys just left me out there to get eaten by the goddamn wolves."

"Sorry, I kept telling them to go back out for you!" Lena gave him puppy dog eyes, reaching out to adjust his hair. He yanked away before she could make contact.

"Forgive me," she said, her voice still soft and placating.

Leander huffed out a breath and ran his hand down the back of his neck. "I fucking *hate* crowds." Then he shook his head and looked around, finally seeing us. He straightened. "Whatever. Let's just get to our suites."

He started our way but Lena put a hand out to stop him. He glared down at where she touched him.

"Who's she?" Lena leaned in and whispered, not even trying to hide her cattiness, apparently. And maybe she thought she was being quiet, but in this big open conference room, her sharp voice carried.

"None of your business," Leander answered shortly, his eyes barely shooting my way to register my presence. At her wounded look, he said with limited patience, "Look, she's just my publicist."

Well. Good to know where I stood.

Lena brightened. She leaned in closer, rolling one of the strings of his hoodie around her finger coquettishly. *Gag.*

"Leander, I've been thinking. You should stay with me for the tour. We can book more security if we're all together cause you can just stay in my suites in each city." She leaned in closer, eyelashes flashing as she blinked up at him. "We both need this movie to do well. And the press goes wild when they think we're together. Even just taking the same flight, *#Lender* has been trending for the last hour."

God, was that really the kind of argument that would win him over? I mean... it wasn't the *worst* PR strategy in the world...

But by the way Leander pulled back, it seemed like it wouldn't sway him. And the fact that I was rejoicing a little inside? Well, I didn't even care if that made me a bad person.

Lena, obviously seeing that she was losing him, grabbed hold of the front of his shirt.

"I'm the only one who knows what the pressure's like." She looked into his eyes. "I can help you." She lowered her voice but I, and I assumed everyone else in the room, could still hear her. "You don't always have to have your brother around. I could be the partner you need. Just look what we did on the movie. I was there by your side. When you got stressed out, I calmed you down."

Then Leander paused and looked down into her beautiful, model-perfect face. And I felt a pang. She was annoyingly perfect. They said beauty was about symmetry, and Lena Clark was as symmetrical as they came. Not to mention she was contoured and made-up as if she was magazine air-brushed, complete with her Cupid's-bow lips shiny with gloss.

She was everything a man like him probably wanted.

And the way she talked about the movie shoot, reminding him of whatever intimacy they'd shared...

I glanced down at my phone and I didn't know if it was the devil in me or what that made me speak up.

I was just doing my job, I told myself later. Giving my client options. It wasn't jealousy. Not at all.

I spoke up from where Janus and I stood, about ten feet away. "I found a place we can get away from the paparazzi. Janus and Milo don't think staying here would be a good idea with as crazy as it is." My voice sounded strange in the sudden quiet. An alto to Lena's soprano.

But Leander turned around to me, and I wasn't sure but I thought I clocked relief on his features. "Oh yeah?" he asked, then turned back to Lena. He chucked her on the chin, like you might do to a little sister. "Thanks for the offer, but that's my ride. I'll see you around the tour stops."

Lena's eyes flashed my way and I could tell I'd just made an enemy.

But as Leander regrouped with the other guys and we prepared to head out to the place I'd found, I couldn't say I exactly minded.

10

FIGHTING OVER...ME?

The AirBnb I found for all of us was... cozy. Certainly more intimate than the 12,000 square-foot mansion the twins had at home.

Everyone had their own bedroom. But there wasn't exactly a maid that came in, or a cook who dropped off ready-made meals like back at home.

So I took the task of cooking for the three grown men upon myself. Which turned out to be a very different experience than cooking for myself and a calorie-conscious teenage starlet.

These men could *eat*.

I had found us a place with an in-house gym, even though we were barely home to use it. Well, at least Janus, Milo, and I were barely home.

We did press morning to night, having to get up at four a.m. for the *Good Morning America* appearance. Janus did that one too. In fact, he did all of Leander's appearances, while Leander squirreled away back at the AirBnb. I hadn't been alone with Leander since... that night in the kitchen, and when we were with his brother or Milo, he barely looked my way.

Maybe he'd been on Ambien that night and had been sleepwalking or something. And had accidentally sleep... finger-fucked me to the first and best orgasm of my entire life? What did I know? I just tried to put it out of my mind and do my job.

Milo hired extra security when we were out during the day, extra cars to help us throw off the paps, and so far, we'd made it back to the Airbnb each night without any hangers-on. The fact that it was in a gated community helped.

Leander only did a few of the appearances himself—ones where he was showing up *with* his brother, and a couple of in-depth interviews with the more serious film reviewers that were asking questions beyond the basic.

Otherwise, Janus took all the other appearances. And I had to admit, Janus was magic with interviewers, both male and female.

He just had this... charisma about him that drew everyone around him in. Except Lena. While they pretended well enough on screen, it was obvious the two couldn't stand each other off screen. She could obviously tell the difference between twins and was in on the secret that Janus did press for his brother. It was pretty hilarious, I thought secretly, how much she seemed to hate Janus.

"So what's with you two?" I asked after Lena all but stomped off after one interview.

Janus looked surprised but then happy that I was actually talking to him. I guess it was a little odd. Most of the time we were so busy, the only one I talked to was Milo unless I was barking orders about where we all needed to hurry off to next.

Maybe it was a little bit to protect myself, too, considering what had happened when I let my guard down around his brother. Still, I was too curious to back off.

Janus grinned at me, angling his body towards mine. I'd noticed he had a habit of doing this, giving whoever he was talking to the feeling that you had his complete attention. Probably why he did so well with the ladies. Unlike Leander, Janus was a total flirt.

Trying to regain my balance, I put a hand on my hip and called him on it. "I mean, I'm just curious. Usually you flirt with anything in a five-foot radius. So what's so different with her? Didn't your brother date her?"

"I don't flirt with anything in a five-foot radius." Janus tried to sound offended but I just lifted an eyebrow. He gave in with a grin. "*Please*, it's a fifty-foot radius, at least. I have range *and* taste. I only flirt with the most beautiful, desirable, and luscious creatures around."

He leaned in with each of those descriptors and I swear, my lady bits contracted with the way his voice curled around the words. Because as he said them, his gaze was trained only on me.

Until he pulled back, his face contorting, "None of which describes Lena Clark."

I laughed out loud at that. "Oh, please. She's America's sweetheart."

"America has bad taste."

I just shook my head, smirking. "Look sharp. You've got the roundtable in ten, and then there's the photoshoot later this afternoon." I smoothed down one of his lapels that had gotten flipped the wrong direction. "There. You look fabulous."

"I look like Leander Mavros. So of course I do." He winked.

I laughed again. It was hard not to around Janus. He was a charming bastard. Too bad he knew it. I shook my head at him. "Save all that charisma for the cameras, Casanova. It's wasted on me."

"Is it?"

I was a little taken aback at the serious tone behind the question. And the way his silver-gray eyes flashed at me when I looked back at him.

For a second, I was caught like that, trying to make out what I saw in his intense gaze that had my heart suddenly pounding.

"Leander Mavros?" An assistant came in through the door and I gasped as I turned away, happier for the interruption than I could say.

"Y'all got this?" I asked without looking back at Janus. "'Cause I'm gonna go grab a coffee. Want anything?"

I took out my phone and still didn't look at Janus. I didn't see anything on the screen. My heart was still pounding too fast.

"Hope." Janus said, and when I didn't answer, again his low voice called, "Hope?"

"Nothing?" I said, pretending I hadn't heard him. "Okay, well I'll be back by the time the round table's over."

And then I fled. If not for my life, then at least for my damn sanity. One brother seducing me with those bedroom eyes was bad enough. I couldn't handle *both* twins being entirely too charming for their own good.

I SUCCESSFULLY AVOIDED BEING ALONE with either Mavros brother for another couple days. They made it to all of their rescheduled press events with a minimum of mobbing. We'd made it through the week in what anyone would call a success considering how we'd effectively stamped down all rumors of the tape and kept the focus just on Leander's movie. And tomorrow was a light schedule before we headed off on the European leg.

I'd just pulled a succulent meatloaf out of the oven and headed downstairs to the weight room to let the twins know dinner was ready. But as soon as I opened the door, I heard a fist on a heavy bag and then one of the twin's voices:

"Damn, brother, leave a little for the rest of us. You aren't the only one who needs to let out their frustration."

I hesitated without meaning to as the other one scoffed.

"What? You? You're out there lapping up all this shit. Lena told me you can't get enough of it." That had to be Leander.

"Oh yeah? Please, do tell me what *Lena* has to say about the situation," Janus returned, sarcasm heavy.

"What's that supposed to mean?"

"What the hell do you think it's supposed to mean? Everyone's talking about the two of you getting back together. You think that's something you maybe wanna run by the rest of us? I thought we were a team."

"We are a team."

"Yeah? Hasn't felt like it lately."

I blinked. I should leave. Eavesdropping like this was wrong... and yet the chance to get some real answers was too tempting. So I tried not to breathe, my hand still frozen on the door knob.

"Who's fault is that?" Leander asked, clearly angry. "I told you from the beginning Geena was a mistake."

"Oh, fuck you. I didn't hear you complaining while everything was good."

Another punch hit the heavy bag. "Things were never *good*." Another punch.

"Weren't they?" Janus pressed.

"Fuck you. Look where it got us."

"It got us here. With a perfect opportunity."

I squinted into the darkness at the top of the landing. What opportunity?

Leander didn't say anything, but I heard the noise of tape ripping, like he was pulling it off his knuckles. Crap, if they were done, they might be coming upstairs. They couldn't catch me eavesdropping like this.

I was just about to pull away when Janus said, "Nope, not gonna let you ignore me on this one, brother. Especially when I've seen the way you look at her."

"Lena?" Leander laughed out loud. "Then you clearly haven't been paying attention."

"You know I'm not talking about fucking Lena."

I'd taken a step back but I froze again at that. Not Lena? Then who were they talking about...?

Leander's laughter cut off abruptly. "No."

"Why the fuck not?"

"Because I fucking said so."

Janus scoffed. "Not fucking good enough. She's perfect. And she likes you. She likes us both. Well, she will. If we give her time. And actually fucking talk to her instead of pulling this hermit asshole thing you've been doing."

"Shut up!" Leander said. "She's a good girl. Just look at her. She was in fucking *pigtails* when we met her. She doesn't do our kind of—"

"We don't know unless we ask."

"I said no. Because we aren't crossing that line again. Now fuck off."

Oh my God, they couldn't be— I mean, was it even *possible* they were talking about... me?

"I'm not letting this go."

But then Leander just roared, "I fucking said *no*," and then

I heard a collision of bodies. Like they were wrestling, and not just the friendly brotherly kind.

"You son of a bitch! I'll take you any day of the week," Janus said, and I heard another smack. Bodies hitting the ground. My mouth dropped open and I was paralyzed. I wanted to run down and get between them, to stop them. At the same time, another part of me wanted to run back to the kitchen because going down there seemed insane. Almost as ludicrous as the thought that they could possibly be fighting about *me*!

"You and Milo think you can run my life but you fucking can't. I'm saying no."

"Stop being such a sanctimonious prick! Oh boo hoo. You're a privileged asshole. Milo and I keep your schedule straight so you can live *exactly* the kind of life you want. But I get some goddamned say in this life we lead too. And this is what's right for us."

"You self-righteous son of a bitch," Leander said. "You think you understand everything because we share DNA. But everything comes so easily to you. You have no fucking idea."

"Poor little rich and famous boy," Janus mocked.

"Wannabe," Leander taunted him back. "Couldn't get your own acting career so you have to take the crumbs you can by pretending to be me whenever you can."

Enough. I didn't care if it was me they were fighting about or not. I didn't know if this was something they'd needed to let out for awhile or what, but I needed to stop them before they said words they couldn't take back.

I flew down the stairs just in time to see the twins circling each other, feet moving in an identical pattern. One had a shirt on, the other, Leander, I assumed, was drenched in sweat, glistening body on display with only a pair of joggers on.

Janus charged his brother with a roar of fury, and I screamed, "Stop! What are you two doing!"

Janus's momentum was already carrying him forward though, so he and Leander collided in a less-than-graceful pile in the center of the weight room floor.

Janus was already trying to pop up and throw Leander off, smiling towards me like I hadn't walked in on him about to eviscerate his own brother. Leander wasn't so distracted, though, and got in a good punch before giving in.

Janus curled over in pain, clutching his jaw as Leander looked up and swore under his breath. "Shit. Sorry, Hope."

"Jesus," came Milo's voice distantly. Janus worked his jaw, eyes watering. "Don't we have enough going on without the two of you beating the shit outta each other?"

Janus held up a hand, "I'm fine." Which might have been more meaningful if his words hadn't come out without any consonants, "I fiii—"

"Are you really okay?" I ran over to Janus and flashed angry, confused eyes at Leander. I was so confused about everything I'd just witnessed. In fact, I was already second-guessing what I thought I'd heard. The issues between them were obviously about more than some argument over a girl, anyway. "Janus?" I asked, putting a hand to his cheek where I could already see a red mark blooming.

But he just grinned up at me. "You can tell us apart. No one can tell us apart."

It was a petty part of me that wanted to say, *Lena can too.* I just looked him over. "Your words are coming out clearer. Do you want me to get an ice pack?"

"Hey, he's the one who came at *me*," Leander said, eyes dark and face stormy as he glared at where I was crouched over his brother.

Janus just kept grinning up at me, blinking a little dazedly.

"You're perfect," he whispered. "Help me up?" He lifted a hand for mine.

"He's fine," Leander repeated dismissively. "I hardly touched him."

Janus scoffed at that as I reached down a hand to him. He took it, even though he barely put any weight on me and I had the feeling he was using it as an excuse to touch me. Especially when he didn't let go even once he was on his feet again. He held my arm as if he needed it for balance, which he obviously didn't.

"My knight in shining armor," he said with a wink down at me.

I rolled my eyes but doubted he missed the flush in my cheeks if the self-satisfied expression on his face was anything to go by. "Yeah, well, it'd be great if you two didn't land bruises on each other. Unless you *like* spending extra time in the makeup chair."

Leander just frowned harder, easily hopping to his feet in a single, smooth motion. Oh, wow. I'd seen him do that on his TV show but thought it had been a stunt double.

"Oh, I'm careful never to leave marks," Leander said in a low, intentional voice, his eyes on me, then dropping down to where his brother still clutched my arm. The way he said it made it sound like a double entendre.

My stomach was doing all sorts of swimmy flips, especially as Leander took a step closer so that I was sandwiched between the two, tall, intensely masculine twins.

My breath caught in my throat as I looked from one to the other, their eyes trained only on me.

"I j-j-j-just came down— D-d-d-dinner's ready," I finally managed to stutter out.

"Perfect," Leander said, eyes dark. "We're starving."

So much promise hung in those words, until, as if fighting

himself now instead of his twin brother, Leander wrenched back from us and turned to jog up the stairs. With a wink at me, Janus led me to follow him.

"He has a sweet tooth," Janus whispered when Milo was out of earshot. "He can only resist a craving for so long."

Why did I have the feeling he wasn't talking about the pineapple upside down cake I'd made for dessert?

11

SURPRISE SURPRISE

After what I'd witnessed last night, I decided the boys needed to let off some steam before Europe. So instead of taking them for a last round of press, together with Milo, I worked out a surprise instead.

"Almost there," I said, barely concealing my excitement as I turned around from the front seat to look back at the twins.

Janus blinked awake from the nap he'd been taking—he hated all the early mornings. Leander looked up from his phone and frowned when he saw trees all around. Manhattan obviously didn't have trees and certainly not forests.

Janus sat up straighter and frowned at Leander. "No seriously, where the hell are we? Milo, did someone pay you off to kidnap us or some shit?"

I looked back at him, horrified. "What? No! I was trying to surprise you two. Milo and I arranged for you guys to have a fun day off today."

Janus just blinked, as if what I'd said didn't register, or maybe he still wasn't fully awake yet. But Leander seemed to have caught on because he was looking around and smiling wide, the first time I'd seen him look actually relaxed since I'd met him.

"For once you aren't in control, brother," Leander laughed, clapping Janus on the back. "So where are you snatching us away to for the day?"

"Didn't you hear the lady?" Milo called over his shoulder. "It's a surprise. So shut your traps and wait like good little boys."

Janus reached up and smacked Milo on the back of the head. A slight problem since Milo was driving. When he ducked out of the way, the car swerved on the narrow road.

"Could we not?" I cried, grabbing for the oh-shit bar.

Leander just laughed, obviously enjoying the chaos that had been delivered into his day. That was good. I wasn't sure how the twins would take the surprise—though Milo promised it would be good. I was a little amused to see Leander taking it better than Janus.

We finally pulled onto a long, tree-laden roadway, *way* off the beaten path.

Late August in LA meant hellacious temperatures and in New York City it had been pretty hot too. But as soon as we parked and stepped out of the SUV here upstate, we were hit by a refreshingly cool breeze that smelled... fresh. Like nature.

Leander was standing beside me, eyes closed, breathing it in. Janus was trying to get a signal on his phone and frowning.

"Okaaaaaaaay," Janus said still sounding skeptical. "You've brought us out to the woods. So no one will hear us scream?"

I laughed. "No! So y'all can let off some steam."

"Trust," was all Milo said as he hopped out of the SUV.

And that was when a man walked out of the small building we'd parked in front of and welcomed us to Rock's Adventure Riding.

"Like horses?" Janus asked, still looking rumpled from his

nap. "Leander is the only one who's trained with horses, so I'll just nope out and stay in the—"

"Horses?" the tall man with a goatee laughed. He looked to be in his late fifties or early sixties, the kind of man who didn't own a shirt that wasn't partially flannel, even in summer. "I thought you understood when you booked what this place was."

"Oh, we do," Milo assured. "My friend's just an idiot."

Janus looked like he wanted to shove Milo again, but that was when the man—Rock himself, apparently—led them to the barn out back.

And when he opened the rickety-looking door, I watched both twins' jaws drop. I glowed with satisfaction at their response. Because inside were six of the slickest looking side-by-side off-roaders.

"We just got a good rain, so the mud should be perfect," Rock said. "There's trails but you don't gotta stick to 'em. Just got some paperwork for you to sign and a quick safety video, then you can head out."

Janus's mouth had dropped open and, as I watched, a glint of excitement came into his eyes. Good. His gaze came my way. "You mean a day of fucking off responsibility and getting to go mudding instead?"

"Uh, fuck yeah." This from Leander.

"Whose idea was this?" Janus asked.

"Hers." Milo pointed my way.

I was still watching Leander, who'd gone quiet as he looked over the vehicles. "If you don't like it, we don't have to stay—"

"Are you fucking kidding?" Janus said. "He loves it. This is like crack to him."

Leander grinned, his warm eyes finally coming my way. It heated me up inside, feeling their happiness and knowing I'd given it to them. "What are we waiting for?" he taunted his brother. "You afraid of how bad I'm gonna smoke your ass once we get on the trails?"

Janus rolled his eyes. "Please. Pretty sure we know who can out-drive who."

"You two are cute." Milo strode forward and yanked a helmet off the wall. "But who gets experience dodging paparazzi every day? Me. You two can enjoy choking on my mud splatter."

I stood off to the side while they all got boyishly excited and crap-talked one another while choosing which ride they'd take. But then Leander noticed me standing by the wall.

"You aren't going to take one?"

I waved my hands. "I hate to admit I'm a cliché, but I'm a terrible driver. I never really had a chance to practice much, and I only handle LA traffic when I'm forced to."

"The side-by-sides have harnesses and a cage around them," Leander said. "Live on the wild side."

I just laughed and waved my hands again. "That's okay. This is for you guys. Go out and have fun."

But Leander looked like what I'd said was an abomination against nature. "Come with me, then," Leander said. "It's a two-seater."

My mouth dropped open, eyes darting to the machine he'd picked out for himself. And as soon as he realized I was even considering it, he wouldn't let it go. I was done for. He grabbed a helmet from the wall and walked over to me, fitting it on my head and standing closer than was strictly necessary while he clicked the strap underneath my chin. His chest was all but against mine.

"There," he whispered, fingertips brushing my jaw. "Trust me. I'll keep you safe."

My breath faltered but I managed to nod. "O-okay."

"God, you're stunning," he whispered, dark gray eyes slicing straight through me. I'd barely blinked and certainly wasn't breathing, when he suddenly pulled back and tugged me forwards by the hand towards the off-roader he'd chosen.

Had I just dreamt that intimacy? And the whispered words? Stunning? Me? I was barely wearing any makeup today. Did he just say that to every woman who stumbled across his path?

I reached up and touched the helmet on my head and tried to remember how to take a breath. "Okay. Well. Then. I guess, um. Okay. Show me how to get strapped in?"

He grinned his million-dollar smile at me. My lady bits melted but then we were moving and I managed to stay on my feet. Ten points for me.

At the passenger side of the ROV, I opened the little door and climbed in.

Leander didn't bother with the door, naturally. He just hopped over the side and landed cleanly inside. I was still trying to get my hormones under control though, so I kept fussing with my harness straps instead of letting him know just how hot I thought the move was.

"Here, lemme help," Leander offered. A thin pretense so he could get close to me again? I couldn't help letting out another sharp little breath as he leaned across me to straighten out the straps I'd gotten tangled.

And every time I did—let out a little breathy noise from his closeness—his eyes would shoot to me. As if he knew exactly what he did to me and was glorying in it, taking his time so he could revel in the moments of tension between us.

Yet he was careful not to touch my body as he clicked the harness straps together. Torturously careful, if the way his dark, needy eyes stared into mine while his strong hands firmly strapped me in, tugging on them once he'd gotten them buckled.

Finally, finally when I thought I might combust from his nearness, he pulled back to buckle himself in. He grinned at me and reached to turn the digital key to the *on* position, then pushed the *start* button. Did he have any idea what he did to me? Or did he just take it for granted that this was his effect on all women? Good Lord!

Whether or not he did, Janus and Milo sped off in front of us, and Leander wasn't about to be left in the dirt. He shifted into gear.

"You ready?"

I nodded quickly, not wanting to slow him down. He took off the next moment, and I was glad I was already clutching the cage bars beside me, knuckles white.

Leander laughed out loud as he hit the pedal harder. And his delight at the wind hitting his face as he accelerated was clear. The man who was always so silent and taciturn was actually laughing. From what sounded like actual joy.

Or maybe he was laughing at me because what I was feeling could not be quite categorized as joy. More like unbridled terror with lots of shrieking, as he sped up to catch up to the others on the uneven dirt path.

Milo was in the lead but Janus was giving him a run for his money. The trees were dense overtop of us but there was a field up ahead. Milo and Janus saw it too. I looked at Leander, who was still grinning like a madman. I'd read up and knew he'd done a bunch of off-roading during his downtime during a shoot in Death Valley. It was why Milo and I had picked this particular activity. I hadn't realized that would make him such a daredevil, though.

Because while the other guys were taking the path to the

field, Leander got a glint in his eye and pulled a sharp left, cutting through the woods to get there.

"Hold on," he yelled as he switched into top gear. He headed straight for the trees. The ride immediately turned far bumpier, but the ROV handled it like a champ, churning up the dirt and brambles beneath. Cutting the angle to the field did the trick too.

I yelped, but then, after a few seconds of fighting the brambles smacking us through the cage, I started whooping once we got to smoother undergrowth and burst out into the field.

I turned to the other guys and gave another whoop. "Suck it, boys!" I hollered.

My energy only added to Leander's, apparently, and now it was on.

He kept the pedal to the metal as we raced across the field. The other guys were out in the open now and flooring it too.

"Are they close?" Leander yelled my way. I still had a hand on the bars but I was finally feeling the adrenaline of it all, laughing along as Leander lengthened his lead. Oh my God, this was thrilling! My hair had pulled out of its tie and was flying wildly around me. I felt it too—wild. Untamed. Ready for anything.

"Milo's gaining," I shouted, "but you've still got a good lead."

Leander grinned with all his teeth, the air tearing at his face, both our blood rushing. And I saw what I'd truly given him today—a gift that money couldn't buy.

Finally, we hit the other end of the field and geared down as we hit the part of the trail that put the *mud* in mudding.

"Oh!" I couldn't help shrieking as we hit the first of the mud puddles, the ROV sliding sideways.

Leander rode the drift and swung the wheel into the turn

at the last moment, swinging us around the next corner. I screeched the whole time, but as mud spewed all around us, it finally turned into a gut-level laugh, and then I was whooping again.

We'd lost a lot of our speed, and we had to slow down more as we rode through a small stream, but then we were off again.

"Go, go, they're almost here!" I smacked Leander on the shoulder.

He laughed, and I decided there and then it was my new favorite sound. "Yes, ma'am," he said, shifting gear and pressing the gas.

Leander and Milo traded the lead back and forth throughout the course, but Leander was back in control as we came back around towards the barn.

My adrenaline had pitched higher and higher the whole ride. We were in the lead. We'd win!

But then, as we neared the last curve, Leander hit the brakes.

First Milo and then Janus zoomed past on either side of us.

"What are you doing?" I cried, smacking the dashboard. "You're letting them get away!"

But Leander was smiling contentedly, eyes on me. "I don't care about that. I want a moment with you."

Leander watched the confusion leave my eyes as I swiped at my mud-spattered face. Which I was pretty sure only achieved wiping the mud across my cheeks more. I was a mess. "Let's go back in, and I can get cleaned up—"

But Leander chuckled and leaned close with his thumb, pausing just millimeters away from my skin.

I swallowed hard, my eyes searching his.

"My heart's beating really hard." I whispered it like a confession.

"We were going fast."

"I want you to kiss me," I blurted, the adrenaline and his closeness and everything making it just pop out. My eyes immediately went wide and I wanted to take the words back.

And then I didn't, because Leander wasn't a man to waste time, and the next second his lips were on mine.

He unlatched his harness and leaned over me, one hand behind my neck as he pulled me as close as my harness would allow. "As you wish."

And then he kissed me deeper still. He kissed my lips softly, so soft I'd never known a kiss could be so tender... or erotic. Then he lifted his cool hand to the skin of my neck, hot and flushed from the heat and the adrenaline of riding.

I reached for him, needing him closer, clutching and releasing at his shirt, scrabbling at the fabric with my fingertips in my need for him—

He groaned into my mouth as he kissed me. "I've always wanted things I shouldn't. And I wanna touch you now, honey. You got other ideas, you say something now. 'Kay?"

I nodded.

"Need your words."

"'Kay," I breathed out, eyes rolling back when he dragged his fingers down my belly and digging them beneath my jean shorts.

I'd worn the short ones today. I didn't care that I was fuller figured. I could still wear short shorts and look fabulous in them. I might be shy but I didn't have to dress like it. It was one thing I'd learned from hanging around the world of the rich and famous.

Which I was particularly happy about at the moment

since it meant Leander had access to my inner thigh. He ran his hand up my smooth skin.

Dear God, the feel of him there. His fingers sank into my skin and he clutched me as he climbed on top of me for better purchase.

And a wanting unlike anything I'd ever felt before came over me. I finally understood it—wanting sex. I wanted Leander over me. Or to climb him. I wanted him inside me. I wanted to feel it all, all at once, God, I *wanted* it—

Instead, his fingers teased me.

His male scent and warm body all around me as his hand massaged nearer and nearer to my center...

12

BARE IN THE WOODS

Leander shifted on top of me in the small space of the ROV, lodging his left knee on my seat between my spread legs.

And at the same time, he'd worked his fingers beneath my pants. I couldn't help my moan, which made him lean in further and latch his mouth onto my neck. His middle finger met my hot, wet, waiting flesh.

Oh God, it felt so good to have him finally touching me. Still strapped in by the harnesses, I scrabbled for him as best I could, frustrated my arms were constrained but not wanting to bother to free them.

Because I could feel him. Through his jeans, he was hard against my bare thigh. All the mystery I'd wondered about forever and there it was. There *he* was.

My hips lifted involuntarily against his seeking fingers. All the muscles of my sex reacted as the sensations he'd only so recently introduced to me sparked back to life.

"I haven't been able to think about anything else except this," he growled in my ear and my sex contracted. I gasped out a squeal of pleasure, near to coming even though he'd only begun to caress me.

I fisted my hands in his shirt. He made me crazy. This feeling inside me was crazy. I was hot inside and out, and I wanted his mouth on mine, and his body on mine, and everything, I— I wanted *everything*.

"Fuck," he growled, pressing his forehead to mine instead, when all I wanted was his lips. I tried to reach for him but the damned harness held me back. Frustrated, I reached for them and fought with the buckles, but his large hands stopped me.

"Don't," he said roughly. "These might be the only things keeping your virtue intact."

His chameleon eyes were silver in the sunlight, burning as he stared into mine.

I was breathless as I stared right back, captivated. "Who says I want it intact?" Then I blinked. "And who the hell says I have any virtue t-t-to—"

But he must not have cared *that* much about my virtue because right then he leaned his whole hand into the crease of my pussy, his thick middle finger sliding inside.

My entire body shuddered against him.

"Leander," I gasped.

"Fuck," he said. "Say it again." His finger found a spot inside me. He made the tip of his finger a hook and then rubbed hard, thrusting with his hips as if he was— As if he was—

"*Leander*."

My fingernails dug into his shirt as I squeezed even tighter around his finger. He thrust again with his talented hand, cock stiff against my upper thigh and I lost it.

It was so good, so so good, better than it even had been in the kitchen. Dear God, that had just been a warm up for this, with his body pressing in against me like this, inhaling him, looking into his eyes between each gasped breath—

"Leander," I squealed again before the blinding light hit my body.

"That's right," he said. "That's right, honey. Let it ride all through your body. Fuck, honey. Fuck, you're so tight, I can feel you coming. That's right. You're so tight. It's so fucking soft in here. Soft but so, so fucking tight. Like nothing else in the world. Fucking incredible."

And then, like he couldn't stand it anymore, he leaned down, finally granting me the kiss he'd denied me before. And he didn't just kiss—he devoured. He kissed like he needed me to breathe. And feeling the steel against my leg, I believed it.

"I can smell you," he broke apart, pressing his forehead to mine again. I was still shuddering from all the things he was doing to my body. His fingers were embedded deep and his finger was pulsing against a spot so deep, oh God, how did he know my body so well when we'd only just—

"And feeling you come apart, it's taking every ounce of willpower not to come in my pants like a goddamned teenager," he chuckled, pressing his cheek against mine. "I want to take you back to the house and fuck you for hours."

I blinked and gasped for breath, but already it was rising again. I nodded, not sure I could manage words. But he was just looking down at me, an unreadable expression on his features. The hand not inside me caressed down my face. Then his grip firmed as he palmed my skull and traced my jaw with his thumb, holding me perfectly still.

"I'll need hours to discover all the places on your body that will make you shudder and squirm. And what kinds of noises you can *really* make." His voice was a hot rasp in my ear. I trembled at the heat of his breath, and that was before his teeth nibbled at my earlobe.

My body pulsed. One hard pulse, like a heart being shocked back to life.

That's what this felt like. Leander was bringing me to life. Because I'd had no clue I could feel this—that life could be...*this*! That sensations like this were even possible!

But then, just when I thought he'd unbuckle me, he pulled back. He did nothing to the hardness that was jutting obscenely from his jeans. It looked painful.

I wanted to see it. To give him even an ounce of the relief he'd given me, and to reveal the mystery. God, I wanted to see. To touch, to...taste, even? I reached for him but he pulled free of my seat. His dark grin said he'd seen my gesture though.

But then his smile dropped as he looked at something behind me and I turned around. In all the, well, all the was overwhelmingness that was Leander, I hadn't registered the noise of the two other ROV's pulling up.

Janus was grinning as his eyes ping-ponged between me and his brother. Miles's eyebrows went up as he brought his ROV to a stop. I looked down at myself. Yes, I was still strapped in to my seat, but my t-shirt was hiked up, barely covering my bra, and my short shorts were still unbuttoned and tugged low.

It was clear what we'd been up to.

I immediately started to straighten up, but Janus's words had me freezing in my tracks.

"Did you tell her how we work?" Janus asked, climbing out of his ROV and hopping over the side instead of using the door, just like Leander had. "Is she in?"

"Shut the fuck up," Leander growled, shoving the door of our ROV open and getting out in the same fluid motion. "You're interrupting a private moment."

Janus just laughed and got right in his brother's face while I scrambled to rebutton my shorts. "Are you sure?" The two of them stood there facing off like identical angry bulls, as if it was only one staring in a mirror out in the middle of the woods.

I finally got the damn harnesses undone and spilled out of the ROV. I yanked my shirt down and tried to get between the twins.

Something I accomplished a little too well, apparently, because Janus was suddenly there in front of me. He pressed me back against the hard wall of his brother. And Leander was still very hard, poking into my ass as his brother caressed my face.

"Hi, beautiful," Janus said, his voice surprisingly tender. "I know this might all be a lot at once. But you're stunning. Nothing happens you don't give the go-ahead to and you can tell one or all of us to fuck off anytime. But—"

And then he dipped down, *his* breath on my ear and neck where his brother's had been only minutes before. It had the same effect, especially on my body that had barely finished orgasming before he and Milo had appeared. I couldn't help the shudder that erupted down my spine.

I gasped and looked behind me at Leander, hoping he wasn't mad at me for responding to his brother.

But he didn't look mad. No, his hand was snaking around my waist and the hardness pressing into me from behind leapt in response, in fact. And then, while one brother kissed at one side of my neck, the other bent low to whisper in my other ear.

"You like that, honey?" Leander rasped as Janus's teeth met my collarbone.

"Mm hmm," I squeaked out, blinking rapidly, feeling too much to do anything but be honest. "I-I-I d-d-d-don't know what you want to hear. But y-y-y-yes mm hmmm. I like it."

"I want to hear what you like," Leander said, fingers squeezing at my waist. "That's all I want to hear, honey. Never lie to me. You like it when my brother sucks on your neck like that?"

I nodded, not trusting myself to verbalize anything. I still wasn't sure I wasn't having some dirty, filthy dream from all the frustration of being around these sex gods day and night.

Especially when Leander reached down and palmed my ass, squeezing, and not gently. "Fuck, you don't know how long I've waited to get my hands on these. Janus, feel 'em. I've seen you looking. Feel these juicy cheeks."

Leander gave another good squeeze even as Janus's hands wandered down my back, slowly, oh so slowly.

Four hands wandering, exploring my body. Outside my clothes, but with an intimacy as if they'd always had rights to access my body. Their hands claimed my flesh as if I was already theirs. Oh *God*, yes. Yes, to feel this way, between them, to have their hands on me like this, I think I'd give anything.

Their hands exchanged places, Janus's finally on my ass. I knew because he groaned low and pulled me to him. Now I could feel his hardness too. Leander stepped up and into me from behind and I could feel *both* of them.

Straining for me. Janus's hands on my ass pulling me up and into him. All but fucking me here in the middle of the dirt path except for the fabric between us.

Which was when I remembered we had an audience.

Feeling my cheeks flaming even as the pleasure spiraled through my stomach, I looked up and saw Milo watching while he had a hand lazily on the front of his pants.

"I forgot to tell you," Leander said, hands massaging my tits and fingers teasing my nipples. "Our other brother likes to watch."

"I need her naked," Janus growled. "Now."

13

BUT SHOULD WE?

"Wait," Milo said, stepping forward, hand dropping off of his jeans. "No. She's a virgin."

My mouth dropped open and I looked at the ground, mortified. I couldn't believe he'd told them— I hadn't even meant to let it slip that night at the afterparty.

Leander's hand came to my face, firmly guiding it to look up at him. "Is that right?"

Mesmerized by his eyes, I couldn't do anything else but be honest. I nodded. But then I reached out a hand and grasped for Janus, who was close. I looked back up at Leander, who was still cradling my face. "But that doesn't mean I don't want this."

Leander's nostrils flared and his arm went around my shoulders, drawing me away from Janus, but only to guide me back to the ROV.

"Back to the car. Now," he declared.

The other two men moved like it was an order from a commanding officer. I was surprised since usually there was such bickering among them. But no, everyone went to their vehicles. I wasn't quite sure what was happening.

One second, I'd been surrounded by hard-muscled men, so hot and horny I'd barely known what to do with myself and the next, here I was—

Being shuffled back into the ROV, Leander deftly redoing the harnesses I'd fought with.

And then we were finishing the track. The three guys thanked Rock and then they were flanking around me, ushering me into the front seat of the SUV.

None of them spoke a single word to me and I felt devastated.

They'd learned I was a virgin and everything had just... stopped. Dammit. I'd been on the cusp of the most exciting sexual experience of my life and it had been ruined because of my stupid big mouth! My heart sank as Milo pulled away from Rock's Adventure Riding. They thought I was still a little kid. They'd go out and seek someone like Geena now. Someone experienced and worldly and sexy and—

"There," Leander said. "Pull off down that little road. It looks deserted enough."

Pull off? I sat up straighter, looking around. But Milo's eyes were only on the road. He pulled off the small local road onto a dirt road that likely led to someone's property. It was deserted and trees canopied the road on both sides.

"What are we—?" I started to ask, but the SUV was pulling to a stop. We were officially in the middle of nowhere now. Milo had parked off *off* road, all but in the trees.

If I was with anyone except these three men, I might be scared. With the tinted windows, no one could see inside. But even though I'd only met them recently, all I felt was excitement. Because maybe...just maybe... they weren't bothered by the fact that I was a virgin?

"Get back here. In my lap," Leander ordered.

"Naked," Janus followed up. "I want to see our prize."

"Did you hear what I told you back there?" Milo growled.

"Oh, we heard," Leander said, reaching forward to help me squirm through the narrow space between the front two seats to get to the back. "And I'm afraid it's only made the prize more precious."

Precious? I'd never been thought of as precious in my entire life. Useful, yes. Sturdy. Good for work or taking care of other people's children, absolutely.

Precious, though? Never.

I started to pull my shirt off but Janus shook his head. Instead, he reached for the hem of my shirt. His fingers skimmed up my soft stomach as he pulled it off over my head.

There was a collective noise from the men as soon as it came up over my breasts. As a full-figured woman, my breasts were... well, big. They were very big. Janus tossed my shirt to the floor, and then his fingers were at my back, deftly undoing my bra.

And when I spilled out, Leander swore. He'd played with my boobs during our make-out sessions, but he'd never seen them in their full glory like this. "Get her fucking shorts off. Now."

I blinked but reached for my shorts. Again, Janus beat me there. His arms reached around from behind, pulling me to his body as his fingers fussed with the button of my shorts. The position had me up against his hardness, and oh, was he fully hard again.

They were taking off my shorts... my heartbeat sped up. Did that mean I'd finally leave this van no longer a virgin? I only felt a little bit of anxiety at the thought. Mostly just excitement. It was time. And maybe it was completely foolhardy and only exemplified my naiveté, but I trusted these men with my body.

Janus dragged my pink cotton underwear down with my

shorts. The SUV was a small space and immediately a certain smell hit the air. My cheeks flamed when I realized it was the scent of my...of my *desire.* Oh God, could they—?

By the way Leander's nostrils were flaring, his eyes shooting to his brother, and then to Milo—

"Change of plans," Leander announced. "Put her over your lap, Janus. Because I've got to taste her this fucking second. She's wet for us and I've got to taste that fucking honey or I'm going to lose my goddamned mind."

14

GIVING IN

Janus sat down on the long bench in the back seat beside his brother and then they were both manhandling me.

I wasn't a small girl but they hefted me around as if I were no more than a feather. I yelped a little in surprise as Leander positioned me facedown over his twin's lap, ass up.

"Spread her," Leander demanded, and oh God, Janus did. He dragged my legs apart, exposing me to—

I turned to look over my shoulder, not an easy feat from where I was facedown near the sliding door of the SUV. But what I saw stopped me in my tracks. Along with the feel of Leander's hands on my back thighs, I watched his head disappear between my legs to inspect my ass.

His fingers squeezed my plump ass, then he pulled me open and I gasped. He was— He was exposing— Everything! I felt cool air in places I'd swear I'd never felt cool air before.

I tried to flip around on Janus's lap, but both Janus and Leander's hands held me firm. Janus's hands clutched my waist, occasionally massaging my back. "Hush," he said. "Ass up. He's going to taste you now."

I blinked, confused but eager to please. Everything happening so far was surprising but not unwelcome. I hiked my ass up as high in the air as I could—a difficult feat since Leander was still spreading me so wide apart.

A strong, stinging slap landed on my ass. I yelped a little in surprise and jumped on Janus's lap. I wasn't sure I liked that. But then Leander landed another and then massaged the places he'd spanked.

And then, oh God, and then—

And then there was hot breath in a place that had never felt hot breath before. His mouth was inches away from my sex—

I arched my back to give him as good of access as possible and apparently that was all the encouragement he needed because then he just started absolutely going to town.

I'd heard about this, sure. A guy "going down" on a girl. Half of me thought it was an urban legend. Yeah, girls gave guys blow jobs, but did any of them ever *actually* reciprocate? I'd doubted how often it happened in real life and yet, here was this man, this *god*, and he was so, so *good*—

And then all rational thought fell out of my head. I scrabbled for something to grab hold of, eventually finding the bottom rung of the seat and decided that would have to do.

Leander's mouth on me was—

Oh God, yes. I was melting. His mouth on me had turned my insides to honey, I was melting. Oh God, I was melting and turning to fire and it was so, so good— How had I lived my entire life without this feeling, this sensation. More than his fingers, the soft texture of Leander's tongue as it swiped up one side of my sex and down the other.

And then he put his whole mouth on me and started to suck.

I screamed.

I couldn't help it.

I screamed out my orgasm, the best I'd had yet. I let go of the seat rung and clutched for Janus's leg. I needed to touch him, to have some sort of grounding in their bodies, and his legs would have to do. I clutched at Janus's ankle, and writhed in his lap, feeling an extra lightning zing when I could feel his hard cock thrusting up against my belly and breasts.

"Enough," Janus said, his voice more deep and gruff than I'd ever heard it. "Leave some for the rest of us. She's driving me crazy writhing on me while you do that to her."

Leander lifted his head, and when I turned mine to look at him, I saw his satisfied grin, face glistening with my juices. "She's a fucking honey fountain. There's plenty to go around. But I know the desperation." He swiped his mouth with his forearm, and it was the sexiest gesture I'd ever seen in my entire life. "Turn her around."

So that's just what Janus did. He lifted me off him, a difficult task, I'd have thought, since I was limp as a wet rag. But he tossed me around just as easily. And then I was facing Leander, ass to Janus.

This was all happening so fast, like something out of a dream. So much so I wasn't sure I hadn't fallen asleep on the drive back and this was an excellent filthy nap fantasy. Except everything happening was so beyond anything my naive little imagination could even have come up with.

And now I was up on the seat between Janus, facing Leander this time. Janus dropped to the floor so he had more room and then *again*, a mouth was on my sex. And though they were twins, they did not do it the same way.

No, whereas Leander had centralized his efforts to the nubbin at the top of my sex, Janus seemed to want to gobble up my entire pussy. He licked and sucked every part of me. The lips. Around the entrance. He didn't neglect the bud, either. But when he plunged his tongue inside my tight little hole—

I about passed out, swaying on the bench. Leander saw and scooted closer so that I was resting on his lap, with his large cock pressing against his jeans right in front of my face. That couldn't be comfortable.

"C-c-can I touch it?" I whispered urgently as Janus continued to work me below. In case Leander hadn't understood what I'd meant, I reached out and rubbed him through his jeans.

His cock reacted to me, even through the thick fabric. He hissed out through his teeth, and I liked that for at least a few moments, I had the upper hand.

"Have you ever seen one before?" Leander growled the question.

"No," I gasped, barely able to get the words out amid the pleasure Janus was bringing me down below. "But I w-w-want to. P-p-please."

"Don't make her beg for it," Milo said from up front, where I noticed that he'd positioned himself best to see the show.

"But I like it when she begs," Leander said. "Only good girls get what they want." Leander's hand came down firmly to grip the back of my neck. "Are you going to be a good girl? Are you going to beg Daddy for his cock?"

His words and what Janus was doing to me—it was too much.

I came. Hard.

And I begged, as I looked up at Leander through my lashes. "Please, Daddy. Please, can I touch your c-c-c-cock?"

A look of supreme satisfaction came over Leander's face, like finally everything was settling aright in his previously troubled world. "Yes, baby girl. You can touch it. Pull it out. I want my cock to be the first one you ever explore. Pull it out now."

"Okay...*daddy*." I whispered the last word, still looking up through my lashes as I reached for the buckle of his jeans. He lifted his shirt and God, he had the perfect manly V.

His chameleon eyes went dark, black as night, but he sat patiently while I fumbled with his belt. The seconds ticked tortuously slowly as I finally pulled it loose and then freed his button.

"Now reach inside," Leander commanded, his voice tight. "Pull me free."

I did as he said. I reached inside his jeans. It was warm there. But nothing to the heated steel that met my fumbling fingers. He groaned as soon as I made contact. I gasped too.

Because he was big. Bigger than I'd expected, I think, though I hadn't really known what to expect.

I pulled him free, though it took some doing, he was so long. He'd grown down the leg of his jeans and I had to work to free him. Finally, his long, fat cock flopped free of his jeans and I could only stare... and salivate.

I had one hand gripped around him. And my fingers didn't even reach the other side. So, propping myself on my elbows, I took him in my other hand too, and bent closer to inspect him.

God, it was so much more beautiful in person than I'd ever imagined it would be. I'd grown up seeing crude depictions of dicks my whole life, of course. Long funnels with big holly berries attached at the sides, scrawled all over restrooms and spray-painted on the sides of buildings. They were nothing to the magnificence in front of me. The skin of it was so *soft*. I hadn't expected that, for it being so rock hard.

And the bulbous head had a little slit in it. There was a drop of liquid there.

Curiosity driving me, I leaned down even further and gave the tip a little swipe of my tongue.

Both Leander and Milo swore.

"How do I taste?" Leander growled.

I blinked up at him, surprised, both hands still clutching him, tighter now. "Salty." I rolled the drop of him I'd licked around on my tongue. "And a little bitter."

Leander chuckled, then glared down at his brother. "She can still make coherent sentences. You aren't doing your job."

Janus said something back, muffled from his face being in my pussy, but then while he suckled on my super-sensitive flesh, he slipped a finger inside me.

I'd been just descending to lick again at his brother's cock, but in my surprise, I took Leander's entire tip in my mouth with a groan of pleasure.

Which made Leander's hand land on my head, his fingers tangling in my hair, gripping with the slightest bit of pain, and I loved it. It was like when he'd spanked me, the tiniest touch of pain only arcing the pleasure even higher.

So I did what felt natural.

I sucked. And suckled. And licked. And worshiped the cock in my mouth. I worshipped Leander in the way I'd longed to. His hands came around mine and he taught me how to touch him, to move my hands up and down his shaft while I sucked him.

I paid attention to the way his stomach hollowed as his breaths got shorter when I really applied vacuum pressure. And when I bobbed down so that the head of him touched the back of my throat. Oh, Daddy really liked that, didn't he?

I bobbed low again and his hands in my head held me there. "Swallow, baby girl. Swallow what Daddy gives you."

I nodded around his cock right as Janus's fingers found spots inside me that brought the simmering orgasm back over the top. I howled around Leander's cock, vibrating it, which was apparently the last straw.

Leander pumped down my throat. He was so far back, I barely tasted him, it just went straight down. I sucked and pumped him, wanting it to be as good for him as they'd made it for me.

And when we were done, messy, sweaty drops of Leander's cum spilling out the corners of my mouth, Janus's fingers still lazily fucking me, Leander looked down at me with a dark, possessive look.

"You're ours, now, honey. But we've only just begun to claim you."

15

WOULD I EVER GET USED TO THIS?

"Wake up, baby," said a deep voice and I blinked my eyes open, confused about where I was. Waking up to find my head in Leander Mavros's lap did nothing to help my disorientation. Until everything that had happened before Leander urged me to lay down for the ride back to town flooded back in.

I tried to sit up, but Leander's heavy arms on my waist kept me put. "Shh. Don't get jumpy on us now, sweetheart. We're almost back to the Airbnb. We're a little later than we planned."

"Gotta be a quick turnaround to catch our flight," Milo called back from the front seat. "I got most everything packed up yesterday. Just grab your shit and get it back in the SUV. Fifteen-minute turnaround."

I blinked and tried to sit up again. This time Leander allowed, even assisted, me. So did Janus, whose lap my legs had been splayed over. I flushed as their hands helped rearrange me between them. Would I ever get used to this? Having two pairs of hands on my body?

They weren't tentative in their touch, either. They touched

my body as if they had every right to it. As if this relationship weren't only hours old, but years. And the thing was… it didn't feel as strange as it ought to have.

It felt natural. Like I, too, had been waiting all my life for this. For them.

Not that I'd ever, ever tell them that. I still wasn't sure I wasn't just some sort of weekend fling for them. Or maybe just a plaything to fuck while they were on tour? But wasn't that what I'd been looking for too? A fun romp to lose my V-card? Sure, this was a little more intense than I'd been thinking, but… My mind spiraled back to the moments before I'd fallen asleep, satiated, in their laps. Their *mouths* on me…*there.*

I flushed hot, then felt cold shivers right after. Dear God, I couldn't let myself get used to this kind of treatment. I was looking for fun, not to be devastated after this all ended. I had to protect myself better.

And yet, as soon as the SUV came to a stop and the boys unbuckled their seatbelts, I couldn't say I didn't *adore* the fact that their hands immediately came back to me, each of them taking an arm on either side.

I'd never felt more like a queen than when I was being escorted by two of the most gorgeous men on God's green earth. It was a tad overwhelming, but I didn't pull away. So much so that once we were finally inside and I got up to my room and closed the door, at last alone, I was appalled when I pulled out my phone and saw what time it was.

Holy shit! Milo hadn't been kidding when he said we had a short turnaround window. Our flight to London was in an *hour*. Yes, it was a chartered flight, but still! We didn't have fifteen minutes to get our stuff, we had five—*if that.*

Running around and shoving the last of my toiletries, makeup, and clothes into a garment bag at least kept my brain too busy to overanalyze what had happened earlier.

Milo must have been wrangling the guys on the other wing of the house, because soon, they too had duffels in hand as they jogged back downstairs.

"Chop chop," Milo said, clapping his hands.

We chopped, and then we were back in the SUV, this time zooming towards the airport. Forty-five minutes later we were pulling up to a private airport on the border of Pennsylvania.

"Now this is what I'm talking about," Janus said with a grin as we stepped out on the tarmac alongside a sleek little Cessna.

"I arranged an upgrade for us," I said, grinning back at them and relieved that our interlude hadn't changed everything between us. Yes, I could submit to them in bed… or the backseat of an SUV, as it were… but that didn't change who I was in my professional life—confident, competent, and never taking my eye off the prize.

"Damn, Lena will wish she was riding with *us*," Janus laughed.

When Leander jogged to catch up to me, a thrill ran up my spine. It was stupid, really. Like the high school football star suddenly paying attention to the school nobody.

I'd been homeschooled until high school, and entering high school while wearing floor-length dresses you sewed yourself… um, yeah, I wasn't the most popular girl.

And the PSAs said things would get better when I was a grownup but this was friggin' ridiculous. Leander frickin' Mavros?

Then the wiser inner me whispered that he wasn't my knight in shining armor and I wasn't a damsel in distress.

But I wasn't marrying either of them. That was the whole point. I needed to stop taking things so seriously. Growing up in church, courting had to lead to marriage and a quiver full of babies and— Blech! I didn't want any of it!

What I did want was a seriously hot fling with a set of badboy twins who know exactly how to touch a woman and light up my every nerve ending.

What I wanted were nights I would never forget.

What I wanted was to discover exactly who I could be beyond the proper young woman I was raised to be. I'd been lied to my whole young life about what the world was and what it wasn't—and about what a woman was and what she wasn't. What I could become and what I very much was *not* allowed to do.

The religious texts I was taught said:

A woman must submit to her parents.

A woman must submit to her husband.

Do not lie.

Do not cheat.

Do not steal.

Do not fornicate.

Do not masturbate.

Do not lust after another, even in your mind.

I'd spent the first nineteen years of my life terrified of every thought I had, absolutely convinced I was going to hell because my thoughts were constantly unruly.

And from what my parents and my church taught me, that meant I was doomed to the fiery pit.

I'd escaped and gotten the job in LA while I went to UCLA on scholarship. And slowly, my world broke wide open.

I'd left behind the husk of my past in so many ways. All that old thinking, cast off.

Except for in the way that felt most important. Most primal.

I needed to exorcise the bad religion from my body and from my blood.

I needed one or both of these sexy as hell men to fuck me

—a thrill ran through me both at the curse and at the naughty image the curse brought forth.

It was all I could think about, even though there was plenty to look at as we climbed the stairs to the private plane. And plenty to look at as we seated ourselves inside the sumptuous plane.

It looked more like a private lounge than the inside of an airplane. I settled myself in one of the chairs while Janus disappeared up front, talking to the pretty blonde flight attendant. I looked away, trying not to feel a pang in my chest. But then I remembered how he'd been at the afterparty. He was a flirt. It was just his way. Just because he said sweet things when we were alone, I couldn't start to think that he—

I turned away from them and sat down in a seat facing the back of the plane. Since it was an overnight flight, with a push of a button, the chairs could lay back and become a bed. And good Lord, I'd had a day. My emotions were all over the place. I stowed my purse beside me and, even though I imagined I wasn't supposed to put the chair in the laid-back position until we were up in the air, I did it anyway and closed my eyes.

But the nap in the car meant it was impossible to sleep. I kept my eyes closed anyway as the pilot's voice came overhead and announced take-off. Then the usual feel of the plane speeding up and the lift of take off that always made my tummy feel funny. Then we were up in the air. I breathed out. Okay. We were in the air now. I'd sleep and wake up and we'd be in London.

I could try to make sense of my crazy life there.

"Look how sweet she is all curled up," a voice said from above me.

"Seems a shame to disturb her," came an identical male rumble.

My eyes shot open, only to look up and see the twins

standing beside my seat, Milo not far behind them, all of them peering down at me.

Leander's eyes were dark gray, matching his polo, but they had an excited edge to them that made my stomach flip.

"No time for sleep, honey. Janus bribed the flight attendant so they'll leave us alone the whole flight. Daddies wanna play."

My eyes widened in excitement right as three pairs of hands started pulling at my clothing, stripping me bare in a matter of seconds.

16

NOT NICE... BUT SEGGSY AS HELL

"We're going to push your limits, Hope. I'm sorry and not sorry at the same time, because I want you to feel things you couldn't imagine before you met us. You see, I've never had a blank canvas before."

Who was this guy? I could only stare up at Leander. This certainly wasn't the quiet, reclusive man I'd met on the first two weeks of the tour. Suddenly he was dominant, and demanding... and I was wetter than I'd ever been in my life.

"O-okay," I said, hating my stammer in that moment. But when Leander smiled darkly, maybe I didn't mind it quite so much.

"Stand up," Leander ordered, and clumsily, I pushed the button to bring my bed back into the upright position of a seat again. I stood up and Leander took my chair, with all the bearing of a king on the throne.

"Janus, get her naked."

Janus's hands were on me in an instant, but he wasn't quick about it. His cool fingers caressed up my stomach as he lifted the hem of my long-sleeved shirt. Living in LA could make a girl self-conscious when she didn't exactly have six-pack abs, and without thinking, I sucked in my tummy.

But Leander smacked my stomach lightly with the back of his hand. "None of that. We want all of you, natural, just the way you are."

I released my hold, then felt immediately embarrassed of my Buddha belly. But as soon as Janus peeled my top off over-head, he bent down and was kissing—my tummy! My squishy, soft belly that belied my hatred of all things workout related.

"Fuck, she's soft, brother," Janus breathed out, grabbing my waist just above my hips and then sliding my leggings—and underwear!—down in one smooth motion.

And just like that, I was completely exposed to the three fully-dressed men, all at 35,000 feet in the air. Dear God, what was next? Did this count as joining the mile high club? ...or would whatever we were about to do next? Even thinking about all the possibilities had me sweating. Though I could only think of admittedly few... possibilities, that is. My imagination was shockingly narrow in these respects, and certainly had never included more than one partner, much less three.

But the three pairs of eyes on me looked ravenous, especially Leander sitting regally on his throne.

"Bend her over me. I need that sweet mouth again. And it's time to show her this is no easy ride. And that I'm not the nice man she's seen on TV." He reached forward and put a hand under my chin, forcing my eyes to his. "It's up to you if you can handle us or not. Be honest. If we're too much, there's no shame in saying so."

I nodded but internally was determined to see this through. He said he wanted my mouth on him and he had no idea how much I wanted that too. In the hours since I'd had my hand on his... on his manhood, it had already begun to feel like a dream. But having him in my mouth, feeling the power of him, his hands dug into my hair—God yes, I wanted that again.

Almost as much as I wanted to feel him inside me. I was tired of them putting it off. I hoped at least one of them would fuck me before we got off this plane. My pussy clenched involuntarily, around nothing.

"Arrange her," Leander snapped, and then Janus's—and Milo's—hands were on me, bending me over the side of my former chair so that my mouth was right at—

I gasped when my cheek grazed the hardness sticking up from Leander's pants. I opened my mouth and bobbed my lips around it through the fabric, which made Leander grab my hair and hiss, "Jesus fuck, woman. Janus, give our naughty kitty ten spankings for that. Always wait for my command."

Janus moved behind me and then his hand was coming down on my ass. I jolted with the shock of each smack. I couldn't explain it. But it was insanely amazing. Janus would smack my ass—which was not petite by any means, and then my entire ass and sex would jiggle in the aftermath.

And if I thought I was wet before...!

I twisted my head to look up at Leander. "Please, Daddy. Can I suck your cock now?"

He groaned, and with adept hands undid his button so that his cock sprang free. "Be careful what you wish for, pet," he said, fisting his cock and directing it towards my mouth.

I suckered onto it, luxuriating in the velvety feel of it, licking and sucking as we became reacquainted.

Which was right when Janus landed another sharp series of spanks. I groaned and squealed around Leander's cock in my mouth, which seemed to pulse and grow bigger every moment.

"Get your fingers in her," Leander said, sounding a bit choked. I gloried at eliciting that response from him. *Me.*

"Stretch her," Leander continued. "Because I don't know how gentle I'll be able to be."

Oh my God! Did that mean he planned to—? Was I really about to finally lose my virginity?

I suckled even harder in my enthusiasm.

"Jesus fuck!" Leander called. "Spank this fucking vixen and fuck her with your fingers. Is she wet? Because the way she's fucking me with her mouth—"

"Oh, she's fucking drenched," Janus answered. "She loves being spanked. It's dripping down her leg."

"Then finger fuck her and get her stretched," Leander snapped as I plunged low, taking him to the back of my throat. Right as fingers entered my pussy.

I howled around Leander's cock, and the sensations rose to a fever pitch. I howled with pleasure.

"Did we tell you you could come?" Leander demanded. "More. Give her more."

So with one hand Janus fucked me, and with the other he spanked me, until he had several fingers inside me and was basically wrenching my hips back to meet his spanking hand by my pussy.

It was so much, all so much, I came again.

Which was apparently Leander's breaking point. "Enough," he said. "She's mine now. We'll take it slow at first." Leander lifted me by my shoulders off his cock, glistening with my saliva. "But we won't go easy."

With all the nerve I had in me, I glared right back at him with one eyebrow lifted and said, "You better not."

Leander never took his eyes off me as he demanded. "Fucking *now.*"

He pressed the button to make the chair lie back into a bed again, and Janus and Milo came on either side of me. I was somewhat used to the two of them manhandling me, but it was still a thrill every time.

The four of us, me naked, in this luxurious plane speeding through the air. Them doing these kinky, fucked-up sexy things to me.

Leander lay down on the bed, his cock jutting up out of his unbuttoned pants.

Janus and Milo were so strong, they lifted me—me!—gripping me by my thighs and my ass, spreading me, and then lowering me down right on top of Leander's girth.

My mouth popped open in a wide O of shock at feeling him there. A man's cock at my wet pussy. He was wet with my saliva and I was, well, yes, fucking drenched, as Janus had so eloquently put it.

Leander's bulbous head fit without too much of a problem, but that wasn't the widest bit of him. No, he thickened as the shaft went down, and I felt him splitting me open. There was a sharp *pinch*.

"Fuck, there it was," Leander breathed out, grabbing my hips and helping to guide me down as Milo rubbed my back. Janus went in for my tits, sucking on my nipple. "I just marked her as ours for good."

Leander stilled for a moment, then when he felt me relax, continued pulling me down his shaft. Gravity helped, but he was still just so *big*.

"I can't believe there's still more," I exclaimed, my hands flying to his chest. I hated that he wasn't naked. I wanted to see his chest, his powerful thighs—all of him. And at the same time, being naked on top of a clothed man except where his cock penetrated my center was also so freaking hot. I felt another rush of fluid burst out to help lubricate his passage. My chest thrust outward at the same time. I felt so turned on and so out of control at the same time. Maybe that was the point of all this.

"That's right," Leander murmured like he could read my thoughts. "Give yourself over to us. Let us have you. You don't have to worry about anything anymore. Give your body to us and let us do with it what we will."

"That's right, honey," Janus whispered from behind my ear, leaning a knee on the makeshift bed. Running a hand down to my ass, he gave it a light pat, then a squeeze. "Give your body over to us and let us make you soar."

He pinched my ass, then with both hands squeezed my cheeks, then pulled them apart, helping to open me up to his brother, who sank in another inch... and then another.

I gasped as my pussy swallowed up the last of him, the knob of his cock pressing up against a pleasure center inside me. I bowed over Leander's chest but he shook his head. "Hold her up. I want to see her in all her glory."

Janus and Milo didn't miss a step. They grabbed my arms and hauled me back up to a sitting position as I straddled Leander, his cock stuffing me.

"Now teach her how to ride me," Leander demanded. "And play with her ass." He looked me straight in the eye. "Because eventually you'll be taking two of us at once."

I gasped, not even able to understand how such a thing would be possible. But Janus and Milo had me again, helping me shift on Leander, back and forth. I felt his fat cock slide inside me, in and out.

My eyes fluttered because, oh God, that was intense. He was a *tight* fit, and apparently, he agreed.

"Jesus fuck, she's so tight," Leander said in a guttural voice, hands coming to clutch my hips as he and his brothers helped him fuck me. "You're gonna die when you feel how tight she is. It's fucking impossible. She's squeezing my cock so tight it's fucking heaven. I'm not gonna last much longer."

Oh God, what would it feel like to have him—finish inside me? I suddenly wanted it more than anything. I squeezed around him with every muscle and I could see he felt it, because his eyes all but rolled in the back of his head. But with what looked like an inhuman amount of strength, he growled out, "Not yet. Off of me, get her off."

Janus and Milo were again Johnny-on-the-spot, and where I had been full moments earlier, suddenly I was empty. I'd been lifted off of Leander's glorious cock, and he was breathing heavily, his giant erection pulsing in the cool air of the airplane cabin.

"Janus," he grunted, getting off of the bed from the side and reaching for me where the boys had stood me up on wobbly feet. "Fuck her and come in this sweet cunt. Now. Then I'll finish her the way I want."

Janus just grinned as he pulled at his belt buckle, bright eyes on me. "You got it, boss."

My pussy pulsed in excitement as he shoved his pants down.

"Ass over the edge again," Leander demanded. "And don't make it pretty. You know how I like to fuck and I want her ready for me."

I was manhandled like a doll, bent over in the same position I'd been for the spanking. And then Janus had my hips in his hands, I felt his cock bobbing against my ass, and then he was feeding himself into my pussy. It was easier passage than it had been with his brother, but I was still a bit sore.

He fit, though. I couldn't see his face, but I could hear the pleasured noises he was making and *God*, did these boys know how to make a woman feel like she was beautiful.

"Goddammit, she's tight. Fuck, you didn't warn me."

"I did."

"But you didn't tell me she was *this. Fucking. Tight.*"

Janus kept plunging his cock, which I suppose I should have known would be equally as large as his twin brother's, up my pussy, and Leander got on his knees and in my face.

"You like that?" he whispered, eyes dark. "You like my brother fucking you? How about I play with your nipples while he sticks that thick cock up your cunt? You were a virgin a few minutes ago and now two men have fucked you."

Janus shoved in the last bit and I squealed, burying my face into the leather of the seat. But Leander gripped my hair and turned my face back to him.

"No hiding from this. From us. That's two cocks inside you, and soon, two loads of cum. Milo's watching. He loves having his hands on you while we fuck you. You'll be covered in his cum too. The way he's looking at you, I don't think he'll be able to keep his hands off you in the long run. I think he's a little in love with you. So's Janus."

Leander's fingers gripped my hair even harder. "Don't expect love from me, little girl. But when I mark you as mine, I mean it. And I'll make you so addicted to this cock," he paused his filthy talk to glare up at his brother, "Harder! Fuck her like you mean it!"

Which Janus was only more than happy to do. If before they'd been exploratory in sex, now Janus was starting to show me what fucking was really like. Janus shoved in and yanked out, his balls slapping my—

"Oh!" I cried out, fingernails digging into the leather cushion.

"She likes that," Janus said, and I could hear the pride in his voice.

"But can you make her come from it?" Leander asked, then reached down my body himself, first plucking at my nipples, then reaching all the way for—

I squealed and writhed on Janus's cock as Leander began to play with what I assumed was my clitoris—that mythical part of a woman I'd only read about but now was, oh God, oh God, now I was feeling up close and personal.

"Enough! Finish inside her. It's been too long. I've got to take her now."

Janus thrust three more times, the hardest yet, and then I felt it—the hot spurt of a man coming inside me.

I felt breathless with it. All of it. Especially since there was no time to process. Because before I'd barely had time to register, again strong hands were carrying me, moving me, adjusting my limbs.

And almost as soon as one slick cock slipped out of me, I was on the edge of the chair with Milo holding one ankle up near my shoulder, and Janus holding the other near the floor. Maybe they'd seen me doing yoga one night to know that I was so flexible, but I tipped back on my elbows right as Leander stepped up, his cock jutting even more angrily towards me.

"This won't be an easy fuck," he warned me.

All I had time to do was nod before he was thrusting into me. My legs curled around him and then the other two grabbed my wrists, pinning them above my head while Leander *fucked* me.

It was nothing to the gentle exploration earlier, which I realized had been all for me, to help me get used to their large girths.

No, this was all for Leander. He wasn't holding back now.

He fucked me with abandon, thrusting me into the chair, but it was clear that wasn't enough.

"You need her on the floor, brother," someone said.

The large man on top of me, fucking me so relentlessly, large cock thrusting in, then pulling out only to ruthlessly shove back in—

I was lifted, only long enough for me to be deposited on—you guessed it, the floor. But someone had laid out a blanket.

Leander was immediately on top of me, a large, hot man.

He fucked like a wild animal, none of his usual gentility or calm presence. And the boys held me down for it. It was the hottest, wildest thing I'd ever experienced. My hips bucked up to meet his, and I watched the intensity on his face as he gave into his drive.

He buried his face in my breasts, biting, sucking. He cemented his body to mine, clutching my ass as his hips pulled back just enough to thrust and bury himself inside me again. It was like he was a man possessed and my body was his salvation, if he could just reach far enough inside me, just fuck me good enough.

I would have clutched him back except for the hands holding my wrists, but I loved that too, because for whatever reason it turned him on; it was what he needed. This was what they all needed, what made them whole. And the fact that I was the center of it was so, so—

Oh God, and not to mention that with Leander's body so close to mine, his groin rubbed *so good* against my spot, so many spots, it was overwhelming, I was overwhelmed—

I screamed as I came like a hurricane.

I screamed and fisted my hands, and then hands were holding mine, and I clutched them and squeezed around Leander, who sucked harder than ever on my neck as he fucked me like a demon was chasing him.

"Milo," he demanded. "Now. On her chest."

He lifted off me only the slightest bit so Milo could step forward.

"Watch," Leander ordered, still fucking me hard. "Watch what you do to us. Look at his cock. Watch what you do to him."

I looked up and there was Milo, usually so friendly and carefree, kneeling and fisting his cock right above us with an intense look on his face. We were all so close, the cloud of sex and sweat in the air. I saw cum dribbling down Milo's cock. His cheeks were bright pink but he kept fisting it, back and forth in a punishing grip. It was smaller than the twins', but then, almost anything would be, but still long and straight.

"I want her covered in us," Leander said. "Mark her. Now."

Milo's eyes drifted up and down the scene of me, bare and exposed and being fucked in front of him. And then his cock erupted in a fountain all over my tits.

"Fuck, yes," Leander growled, his hand immediately spreading the cum all over my breasts, bringing it to my lips.

"Suck," he demanded.

I took his fingers into my mouth, sucking eagerly. Which was apparently the last straw.

He fucked me ruthlessly as I sucked his best friend's cum from his fingertips.

I watched as his orgasm hit, and it made another hit for me. All of his features twisted as if in agony, and then every line of stress disappeared. Then he collapsed on top of me, still thrusting with his hips as if he couldn't stand to be done fucking me.

"Fucking mine," he mumbled, before rolling to the side so he wouldn't crush me with his weight but pulling me with him so that we were still connected, his cock still inside me.

Janus laid down on my other side.

"Fucking *ours*," Milo said, sitting at my head and playing with my hair as my eyes drooped. I never imagined the floor of a plane could be so comfortable. But when sandwiched in between such warm, hot bodies that had just taken me to the edge of nirvana...

"You better fucking believe it," Janus and Leander mumbled at the same time.

17

STIRRING THE POT

London was big and beautiful and I felt beautiful in it. And that felt amazing. Like I was walking on air.

Or maybe that was just the residual feeling left in my body after that insane plane ride and all the things—

Oh God, waking up in their arms...

Because we'd slept that way, on the floor of the plane, all tangled up together. Milo woke us all up half an hour ahead of landing. None of us had moved, in spite of the luxury of the plane around us. I'd woken just where I'd fallen asleep on Leander's bicep and never slept more soundly. When I finally stood up, I thought I'd have aches and pains, but instead I felt loose and only achy in the places where— Well, ahem, in places that had nothing to do with how I'd slept.

I'd had time to clean up in the bathroom before buckling back up for landing and then we hurtled back into the craziness. Being hustled through the airport by our UK bodyguards while crowds were barely held at bay—it made everything that had happened on the plane feel even more surreal, more impossible.

Surely I hadn't just been de-virginized at 35,000 feet? By

the sexiest men on the planet? God, it all but took my breath away to remember it. The hands caressing my body. The fury that Leander had taken me with, claiming me like I was some kind of salvation—

What was crazier? It had sort of... worked. I mean, Leander was like a different man as soon as we stepped off the plane.

The moodiness had disappeared. And right now? It wasn't Janus pretending to be Leander that Graham Norton was out there interviewing. Nope, it was Leander himself, along with Lena and some other British actor that I didn't recognize. And Leander was killing it. The crowd was eating out of the palm of his hand. He'd just told some joke about on-set hijinks that had the crowd laughing their asses off.

Janus and I were watching from the green room. They really did have everything you could want in these places—a fully stocked mini-bar and craft services trays of little sandwiches. We'd filled little plates and grabbed sodas when we'd all first come in, hanging out together before an assistant had come for Leander.

Milo went with them to stand by on set and make sure Leander had everything he might need.

...which left me all alone with Janus.

I thought he should sit in the audience, but he'd waved me away and said he wanted the night off if he could get it. I thought I understood, since Leander going on as himself was a rare-enough occasion.

Janus was different on his own than I thought he'd be, though. The buoyant, gregarious guy I usually knew was absent. He was pensive. Pacing, even, while he watched his brother.

"You okay?" I asked. "He's doing fine. Great, even."

Janus gave a quick, half-shake of his head. "It's not that."

But before I could ask what it *was*, he'd grabbed the remote and was turning up the volume. I reached for my soda and took a sip.

Just in time to see Lena put a hand on Leander's thigh as she leaned over him to whisper to Graham Norton, "Fine, we'll tell you, but just you. Yes, we are back together."

"The fuck?" Janus exploded right as I spit out the bit of lime soda I'd just sipped through the straw. I frantically swiped at the front of my shirt as Janus turned the volume up even higher.

"And now is the part where you deny it, fucker," Janus said to the TV, glaring at Leander.

The camera focused in on Leander's face for a closeup, Graham and everyone in the studio audience waiting for his reply. Along with Janus and me.

But Lena continued before he had a chance, and the cameras quickly panned back to her, "We've been back together for awhile now, but the paparazzi can be monstrous. Well, I don't have to tell you British folks about that." She furrowed her eyebrows sorrowfully and Graham did the same, putting a hand to his heart.

Then her expression changed, brightening to a beauty pageant grin as she forcibly clasped Leander's hand in hers and posed for the cameras. "But we're choosing to trust in the good of humanity. And frankly," she laughed, "we just can't keep it a secret anymore."

Graham Norton's eyebrows went up. "Oh? Is there another big announcement coming then?"

Leander's face was impassive, completely unreadable as he looked intensely down at Lena. He also didn't say anything to negate her *big news*. She just giggled and was clutching his whole arm now.

"Oh hush, no, don't be starting rumors now." She laughed

some more, that annoying high-pitched laugh that made me want to gouge her eyes out *just* that little bit more than I already did, and that was saying a lot. "We're just announcing we're a couple, that's all. For *now*, anyway." More eye-gouge inducing giggling.

Then she turned her head towards Leander and went in for a perfect movie kiss.

I grabbed the remote from Janus and turned the TV off, then spun away from the set where it was hung on the wall.

"That wasn't what it looked like," Janus said, immediately jumping to his brother's defense in a way that pissed me off for some reason. "You know Lena's a scheming little bitch. You could tell she ambushed Leander—"

I didn't care. I was furious. So like the goddamned little brat that I apparently was, I took three quick steps forward, threw my arms around Janus's neck, and kissed *him*.

18

BRATS GET WHAT BRATS DESERVE

Janus's lips were hard against mine, and he immediately snatched my arms from around him. He hauled me backwards into the open space of the room, between the couches.

The dark anger in his eyes told me I'd screwed up.

No, let's call it what it was—I'd fucked up. I'd done fucked up.

"I'm s-s-s-orry," I stuttered out.

Janus just grinned, his fingers tightening for a moment on my wrists before releasing me. His eyes burned a bit darker, I thought, as he stepped back into me to whisper in my ear. "Oh, not yet, brat, but you will be. I'll make sure that little ass of yours feels very, very sorry by morning."

I wrenched back from him, suddenly angry. "Look, I don't know how this works. You—" I looked around us and lowered my voice. We were the only ones in the room and it should be private. "You had your"—my eyes dropped down below the waistband of his jeans—"*you know*, inside me yesterday. And today we can't even kiss?"

I tried to reach for him again, and again, he caught my

wrists. "There are rules," he growled out. "And Leander sets them. He says when. He says how."

My mouth dropped open in surprise. "And you're okay with that? Since when do you let him run the show? You never stop giving him crap, and you challenge him all the time."

"It's the nature of a Gemini," Janus smiles. "We don't just look alike. But we're plenty different too. He needs to be in control."

He smirked at me, stepping closer into my space. "I don't. We have different needs."

"Such as?" And I really wanted to know. I wanted to understand, if only to get a better feel for what the hell was going on around me. How had my world gotten so upended so quickly?

"When Leander's running the show, I don't have to control it anymore. It's the one place I can let go completely. He'll take care of you, me, Milo. And it makes him better to handle the rest of the time."

I arched an eyebrow, still feeling frustrated and pissed. Leander got to go out there and kiss whoever he wanted but Janus and I had to wait for his say so? Sounded like BS to me. "Oh, and you get nothing out of the deal? You do it all from the goodness of your heart?"

He reached out and grabbed my ass, pulling me to him by my ass cheek and a hand on my inner thigh, thumb brushing my pussy through my leggings. He sat down on the couch and spun my body, positioning me in front of him ass first.

"I didn't say that," he growled. "God knows I want back inside this hot cunt the second he says I can."

"So?" I bent over a little, arching my ass into his hands. Having his hands so close to my... God, it made me feel dangerous. "Why don't you take it?"

They'd opened up an entire new universe to me. How had I gone so far in this world and not known that my body could do these things? I wanted more and I didn't care if it made me greedy.

Janus spanked me and I yelped.

He grinned in response, then reached up to grip the hair at the nape of my neck, bending me back awkwardly to look over my shoulder at him. "Because unlike you, I'm a grown-ass man who knows how to wait. That's why I'm Daddy and you're—"

He rolled my hefty ass cheek in his hand and then smacked it again, and by his face I could see he relished in the way it jiggled. "That's why you're Daddy's naughty little slut."

He spanked me again and I couldn't help my high-pitched squeal, though I immediately threw a hand over my mouth. Good God, we were in the green room of a very posh TV studio. But it was *shocking* how good being spanked felt... at least when they were delivered by this man who knew exactly what he was doing.

Janus squeezed my flesh tighter in his grip. "That's the deal. Leander calls the shots. I enjoy meting out the punishment, Milo likes to watch. Though"—he gripped harder than ever and rolled my ass cheeks in his hands—"we've never had anyone like you before." There was something in his voice.

"A-a-and it's always been like that?" I asked, trying to get information while also trying to keep my thoughts together in any sort of semi-coherent manner. I was just another cog in their machine. I couldn't let myself start to think different, no matter the sweet things that might slip out of their mouths on occasion in the heat of the moment.

His thumbs moved so that he was plunging towards my asshole and spreading my cheeks, the thin fabric of my leggings and underwear no match for him. I could barely stay on my feet with the things he was making me feel.

"I've always liked to fuck nasty," he said, "but it wasn't until

I started fucking with Leander that I understood what sex could truly be."

His thumbs plunged even deeper as he pulled my ass wider to give himself more access. "I don't know what made us such kinky bastards. We were handsome little fucks, and celebrities, so pussy always came easy. We had bitches flashing their tits at us and offering us free pussy from the time we were teenagers. Grown women, and the ignorant little fucks we were, we took it."

I turned around, serious. "That's child abuse."

He shrugged, grabbed my body, and pulled me back to him, down on to his lap now. "Didn't feel like it at the time. You feel like you're thirty, that's how everyone treats you. A hot chick offers to suck you off, what's it to you that she's in her late twenties and you're fifteen?"

"Jesus! Janus, that's not right."

He nodded. "I think I get that now. Seeing other kids come up in the biz and how young they are. But when I was in it, I felt like such hot shit. I thought I had everything handled, you know. That I was in control of everything. I was doing coke so I barely slept, was reading scripts nonstop, developing like four projects at once—" He broke off and stared into the middle distance.

"And then you were arrested for drunk driving."

He looked at me and started laughing, caressing up my inner thigh and manhandling me like he had all rights to my body. His other hand was still possessively wedged between my ass crack, fingers tapping against my pussy through my leggings.

"Don't you mean when I was arrested for driving my Aston Martin into that nice old lady's living room? It was a miracle everybody walked away from that alive."

"So..." I dare to ask the question everyone my age has

always wanted to know, straining not to squeal or stammer at his fingers against my flesh. "Was that why you walked away from acting?"

Again, he shrugged. Never one for an easy answer. "Maybe. I just realized that I couldn't handle that kind of pressure. And that maybe I wasn't meant to be the one out under all the spotlights. Leander had always been the really talented one. While I'd been out partying, he'd been in acting school, really working on honing his gift, ya know. It just made sense for me to take over in a managerial role."

I stared at him. "But why stay at all? Why not go back to college? Do something else completely?"

"What, you gonna give me the same bullshit the gossip rags do about how weird it is that I'm so close with my brother?" He leaned in. "Especially now that you know just how close we can get?"

His voice was a rasp when he said, "We like to be inside the same woman, at the same time. It makes me hard when I get ordered to fuck a woman and other people are watching." He trailed his hand up my neck and then gripped his hand in my hair like Leander always did. It felt strange coming from Janus but just as thrilling.

"I like to feel the insane tightness of a woman coming while my brother fucks her cunt and her ass squeezes my cock. That's going to be you soon, princess. Is this ass going to be ready for me? Maybe we should start preparing it? Hmm, what do you think?" His voice dropped deeper and deeper with each word until I felt them reverberating in my pussy.

And then, right then and there, he spit on two fingers, yanked my leggings and undies down, and plunged his fingers towards my little puckered anus when—

"What the fuck do you two think you're doing?" Leander's voice rang out. "Without my permission?"

19

CHASING OUT THE DEVIL

Leander looked livid as he stormed into the green room, Milo right on his heels.

Milo shut the door immediately behind him and I sprang off of Janus... or tried to. But his hand was tangled in the back of my leggings, fingers circling my anus, and apparently, he wasn't about to pull back.

"You got something to say to me brother?" Leander spit out. "Because I was just humiliated on international TV. And instead of coming back and finding my manager and publicist brainstorming ways to fix this clusterfuck, I find you trying to get your dick in her ass since it's the only cherry left."

With difficulty, I struggled to climb off of Janus, because Leander wasn't the only one pissed.

"You kissed her!" I cried indignantly, crossing my arms over my chest and feeling stupid even as I finished, "So I kissed him."

It was childish logic and there had been more to it, I'd swear, but my brain and tongue were tangled by the last twenty-four hours, and I couldn't say anything right.

Behind Leander, Milo smacked himself in the face with a

hand as Leander's eyes shot to Janus. If he'd looked pissed before, it was nothing to the devilish haze that fell over his eyes now. Crap, I'd said the wrong thing.

"I didn't mean that. He told me how he's just the spanking Daddy and that you call the shots," I said, trying to fix things.

"Did he?" Leander said, voice sharp and caustic. "So why did I just walk in on him trying to stretch your ass so he could fuck it?"

"Oh, that's not what he—" I started, looking towards Janus to back me up, but he was just glaring down at the floor. Wha—? Had that really been— Was he just going to start with his finger and then try to put his cock in there? Inadvertently, I clenched my butt, tensing at the thought.

I looked at Janus again. He'd met his twin brother's eyes, and they were darker than I'd ever seen.

"What the fuck was that with Lena?" Janus spat.

Leander's mouth dropped open. "You know what she's like. She ambushed me with that—"

"Obviously," Janus said. "But you could've shut it down right away. You just let that bitch keep on babbling instead of manning up right then, right there."

"What did you just say?" Leander took a menacing step forward.

Janus gave my ass one last squeeze, then pulled his hand out of my panties. "What I'm saying is that we finally have what we want. Don't go fucking it up by letting that bitch interfere."

"I'm not," Leander said, jaw clenched so hard I thought it might crack. "I'm handling it. But I have a movie I need *not* to tank at the box office because I can't keep my shit together on national TV, when I barely skirted the last scandal. I kept my cool. It was what we all needed."

"And now #Lender is trending on Twitter again," Milo added helpfully from behind us, glancing down at his phone.

"Shit," Leander and Janus said at the same time, then glared at each other.

A knock came at the door.

"If it's Lena, send her away or I'll wring her neck," Janus shot out.

I scurried to the door and opened it two inches, peering out. My heartbeat ratcheted down several notches when I saw it was just a delivery person. I took the paper bag from him and signed. "Thanks."

I shut the door and stepped back to the three men staring at me expectantly. "Not Lena," I said cheerfully.

"What's that?" Leander demanded of the bag in my hand.

I felt my cheeks flame. "Oh, I just got a prescription filled and we didn't really have time to stop. So I had a delivery service pick it up for me."

"What prescription?" Leander demanded at the same time Janus asked, "What's wrong?" and Milo, "Are you okay?"

I waved a hand, my cheeks flaming hotter. Seriously, could this have arrived like an hour sooner or later? Any other moment than right now?

"It's nothing to worry about," I waved them off. "Just the morning after pill, since we didn't exactly, um," I looked at their questioning eyes, then to the floor, squeaking out the last bit, "use protection on the plane."

Silence.

More silence.

Even more silence.

I couldn't stand it any longer so I started to just blurt out words, and more words, any words that came into my head. "You know, 'cause we were all in the moment, and maybe ya'll haven't thought about it. But I'm clean. I swear! I can have doctor's results sent to you to prove it; I know it was irresponsible not to talk about it ahead of time but it was all so fas—"

But Leander just strode forward and grabbed the bag out of my hand. He ripped it open, then pulled out the medication and attached paperwork. His eyes jerked back and forth as he read the fine print, then he shoved it all back in the bag and tossed it to a nearby chair.

"It says you have three days to take the pill. Which means I have twelve more hours to fuck you with enough buffer for safety. Why are we wasting time with anything else? Janus, Milo, spread her. You know what, forget you. I've had enough of dealing with other people frustrating the fuck out of me. It's time to take what's mine without any other fucking bullshit."

And with that, he unbuttoned his pants, spit on his hand and came towards me.

He grabbed me by my throat and shoved me down on the couch by Janus. My head landed in Janus's lap.

"You can both just watch while I bareback our little slut. And dream of how it feels to fuck her raw, 'cause yesterday was your one off, brother."

Leander yanked down my leggings, dragged me underneath him by my hips, and his huge cock was suddenly there between us. He tossed one of my legs up by my shoulder, and then he was plunging in. I gasped at the intrusion, angling my hips to adjust to him even while my sex pulsed at the weight and stretch of his thick, hot, velvety—

"Feel that? There's nothing between us," Leander groaned, sheathing his bare cock in deep while his brother yanked my hair back, forcing me to look up at him.

He was big—too much, and I was sore, and I hadn't really stretched—

"Take me," Leander demanded, pushing in, and it pinched, and he grabbed my ass and pulled me wider open as he continued to relentlessly feed his anaconda cock inside me. And then he thrust home, thick and stuffing me full, him inside me.

Nothing at all between us, skin to skin.

I looked up at him, all my defenses blown away by this man.

"Why did you kiss her?" I whispered, tears cresting.

His chameleon eyes turned from dark gray to silver. "Watch the tape back, baby. I didn't. She tried, but I turned to the side. Knowing how to work a camera angle is my job, babe. But if you look closely, you'll see. Her lips didn't touch mine."

A gush of wetness between my legs gave him passage for the last bit and he slid home with a grunt, balls slapping my ass. Then his hand came to my throat, the brief moment of softness between us gone as he fucked me rough, rough as a devil.

And whatever demons he was trying to chase away, I clutched my flesh around him to help send them back to hell. Because I'd do whatever it took to keep this confusing, dominating, thrilling man right here on earth with me, doing these delicious things to my body while he continued to seduce my soul.

When he buried his face in my breasts to stifle the noise of his roar as his cum flooded my insides, Janus started thrusting three fingers in and out my mouth and I couldn't help wondering...

Did he wish it was *his* bare cock stuffed in one of my holes right now instead of his twin's?

20

BOTH BROTHERS NOW

I was sleeping when voices woke me.

I'd taken to the guys' bed when we got back at the hotel. After the studio, we'd come straight home considering how jetlagged we all still were. I'd collapsed on the bed as soon as we got in. I'd expected the guys to climb in with me and for us to continue what we'd started at the studio, but I must have fallen asleep.

Hearing their voices now, though, I stayed still, especially when I realized I was the topic of conversation.

"And I told you, she needed to be punished, but then you came in and fucked her, destroying everything I was trying to establish."

"We're working with a timetable here, brother," Leander snapped. "I can only safely ride her bare for about twelve more hours before she has to take that pill. The last thing we can afford is to knock anybody up, so we'll give ourselves a buffer."

"You know very well I could have finished my punishment and *then* you fucked her. She was a brat, and brats get punished."

"Oh, I assure you, getting fucked raw like that wasn't easy." I could hear the grin in Leander's voice.

"You're missing the point." Janus sounded furious. "You undermined my authority with her."

"Like you're undermining my authority now? I thought you were the one pushing for this arrangement? So why are you being a little bitch now?"

"Just because I beta in the bedroom doesn't mean you get to push this shit outside of it, brother. And are you seriously going to keep that bare cunt for yourself? I felt her bare too, and I want more."

"Getting selfish, brother?" Leander bit back. "That's not like you. I thought you were the one who was all Kumbaya about this shit."

"Well, both of you are dumb shits," Milo's voice chimed in, "'cause she's been awake for the last five minutes listening to every word the two of you have said."

"What?" the twins said in that identical way they had. Except it was less amusing when you were the one who'd just been caught.

I opened my eyes and lifted my head from where I was tangled in the bedsheets. Jet lag had finally caught up with me when we got back from the studio. It was light out, but that didn't mean much. I barely had any idea what time it was here unless an alarm was going off reminding me to rush us to one appointment or another.

"Sorry, I was just waking up," I said meekly as I lifted up off the pillow.

"That's it," Leander said. "Enough fucking bratty behavior from you." He looked to Janus. "Tie the little brat up and let's show her what happens to brats who try to get away with things. We've given her enough time to sleep."

And then Janus lifted a belt from one of the suitcases he'd

brought with him. A grin settled on his face. "Fucking finally. Let's see how much we can make Daddy's little slut squeal."

Milo chuckled. "I'll get the lube. She's gonna be sore after earlier."

Leander shucked his jeans and underwear, yanking his shirt off over his head by grabbing it from the back, in one swift motion. In seconds, he was completely naked.

I blinked, feeling dizzy from the sight of so much male perfection up close. I— He was—

God, I'd never seen him naked before. We'd done so much, but there'd always been a public element to it. Part of me had been worried I'd never see them naked. That it was some fetish for them, that they liked never letting me see—

Oh, but they were letting me see all of them now, because Janus had done the same, stripping all the way down. And Milo followed suit.

I instantly became wet at the sight of them.

Well, I became wet... down there. Because my mouth? It dried right up and I couldn't get a word out. I just nodded and then nodded again. "Yes, please. *Daddies*." I whispered the last word.

Leander caught my chin under my jaw in a rough grip. "Say it again, little slut."

"Daddy." It was still a whisper, but the way Leander reacted, it might have been a roar.

"Beg for Daddy to fuck you bareback." He held his thick shaft in his hand. "Beg for it or I'm not giving it to you." He rubbed it over the lips of my sex and my buttocks clenched. I lifted off the bed to get closer to him but then Milo and Janus were suddenly there—Milo at my head and Janus at my ankles, holding me down.

Leander loomed over my body like a crouched wild cat, ready to spring. "I. Said. Beg. Daddy. Like you mean it."

"P-p-please, Daddy!" I said but he just shook his head, his grip of my chin getting even crueler.

"I don't think she means it." Leander looked up at his brother.

"I do!" I assured.

"String her up," Leander ordered, straddling me so that his cock laid on my thigh, cradled right against my sex.

Which was when I realized that Janus had not only been holding my wrists, he'd been securing something around them. Padded leather cuffs.

"Up with her. On display. And then we fuck her till she can't remember any name other than Daddy."

Milo pulled some rope I hadn't realized was attached to a pulley system rigged at the top of the four-poster bed. And then I, too, was jerked to a sitting position, with such ferocity that Leander's cock thrust inside me.

Which was when several things occurred to me:

Milo had offered to book the hotel here for a reason—it apparently had special accoutrements, such as whatever sex apparatus I was now attached to. They'd obviously been saving it as a surprise for me.

And whatever upper hand or handle on the situation I might've thought I'd had, I'd been sadly, sadly mistaken.

"You can fuck her ass, brother." Leander smirked as I was hoisted fully upright, arms stretched up and out over my head like I was on a cross. "But you never get to go bareback again."

I clutched the thick rope holding the padded cuffs around my wrists as I was lifted just above the bed. One knee barely touched but Leander was quickly repositioning me, getting on his knees and moving his cock to plunge in again while we fucked face to face. Except that I was suspended in front of him like some medieval torture subject.

"I told you we wouldn't be easy with you, baby," Leander

said, cradling my face as he stuffed me full with his cock. His features twisted in that ecstasy that looked like pain as he bottomed out inside me. "Fuck, you're bringing me back to myself," he gritted out through his teeth, eyes closed.

Eyes still closed, he growled at his brother. "I need her stuffed fuller. I need her to feel the pain of pleasure. Janus. Get a condom on, lube up, and then get the fuck in her ass. We've got her trussed up like the fucking prize she is."

His eyes popped open and I clutched the rope, struggling to understand and catalogue one sensation before another hit.

I glanced back at Janus and saw him with his huge cock out. He had a little bottle of something out and he poured glistening gel on his fat dick.

Then he climbed on the bed behind me. His left hand caressed down my side. And then I felt him there—a cock where his fingers had been before Leander came back in the room so mad.

"Wait, did you put a condom on, you bastard?" Leander asked. "I told you I'm the only one who gets to go bare—"

Janus's hand gripped tighter on his cock and then his breath was caressing the back of my neck. "Relax and take me honey. Your body can handle it, I promise, but you have to relax."

And then there was an inexorable pressure pushing in from behind.

I squealed as I was pressed between the twins, speared by Leander's cock as Janus' shaft stabbed me relentlessly from behind in a place I'd never—

I flung my head back. "Oh God," I cried. "Oh God, oh God."

"He can't help you here," Janus said. "We're your gods and you have to take what we give you."

"Dammit," Leander swore, but then his hands were on my hips, massaging me, his cock pulsing inside me.

Tears squeezed out of my eyes and then he was kissing me. Not hard, though. He kissed me as gentle as his brother was rough, pushing in and in and *in.*

"It's rough, I know," Leander whispered between drugging kisses. "It's too much, almost." His lips dipped down softly on mine. How could a man with such sharp, rough edges kiss so impossibly soft? "But you can take it. I know you can. You're so fucking beautiful and you can take both of us. Soften and take my brother's cock up your ass."

He kissed me deep again.

I clung to the ropes. I kissed Leander back. I tried to relax the muscles in my ass but just ended up clutching tighter. Leander was so deep in my pussy and the pressure *back there...* it was— I never knew anything could feel so— Would he even fit—?

Janus grunted as pain flashed through me, even as Leander's cock massaged the spot inside me that he knew was so *good—*

"Beg us," Leander whispered, his teeth nibbling on my bottom lip. "Janus just got past the first ring of muscles in your ass. It'll be easier now. So beg us to fuck you. Beg us like Daddy's little slut that you are. Beg us both to fuck you."

Tears ran down my cheek. I was too full, so full. I hurt, and I soared, and I—

"Fuck me, Daddies," I squealed and then buried my face in Leander's chest.

"Daddy's gonna fuck you," came Janus's voice from behind me as I felt his hands join Leander's on my hips. "And I'm not my brother. I don't go easy. I'm gonna make it so you can't sit down for a week without remembering who took your ass, and who took it raw. And then I'm gonna pump my cum into you and you're going to fucking love it. You're going to beg me to take your ass and I'm going to teach you to love it when it hurts."

And then he shoved home deep, so deep that I was shoved against Leander, sandwiched between them tighter than a sardine. I screamed into Leander's chest as Janus really started fucking me then, sawing in and out of my ass ruthlessly.

Leander's cock in my pussy steadied me, anchored me.

I gave myself up to them. Gave into the pain. Gave into the pleasure. Trusted them with my body completely.

And sank deeper into my body than I'd ever been before. I sank down and down, a calm roar taking over in my mind as they fucked me into submission.

It was the most beautiful thing I'd ever felt.

It was also when I started coming like a freight train.

It didn't hit hard at first but came on stealthily. But then it rose higher than anything I'd ever felt before—even what the twins themselves had made me feel. No, now I was soaring right past the highs they'd made me feel, to a height so sweet and pure, so torturously pleasurable that I couldn't even make a noise other than a whine, so high-pitched it was barely audible.

And the twins kept fucking me through it, pushing me higher and higher until I escaped my body completely and I felt like a being of white light. I arched and my toes curled and I lived in ecstasy for a moment longer, and then another. And another.

When I finally fell back to earth, it was to find Leander staring at me incredulously while Janus fucked me like an animal from behind. He'd stretched me with his vigorous fucking so it didn't hurt anymore. It was just an amazing, sexy fullness back there. I had no idea I could ever find anal sexy, but dear God it was. It *so* was. Especially while Leander fucked me at the same time.

"Come," Leander demanded. I blinked up glassily at him, my body spasming in response to his command, only to find he was glaring at Janus. "Or get the fuck out of her. She's had enough."

I had no idea what Janus's face looked like in response. Either way, after another few fast strokes, Janus wrapped his arms around my waist, shoving between me and Leander, and buried himself as deep as he could possibly could. He also leaned in and whispered, "I hope you enjoyed your punishment, sweet little slut. Because it's only the first of many."

21

MORNING WOOD

The next two weeks in London flew by in a whirlwind of press events, including an extravagant premiere night.

Thankfully, the night went as planned with no scandals. All four of us even got to watch the whole movie sitting side by side—including playing barefooted footsie in the darkened theater during the latter half. That got me more than ready for the raunchy sex we'd have later that night—

Uh, yeah. London was bananas. I couldn't get enough of the boys...my *Daddies*... and they couldn't get enough of me.

Every free moment we all weren't passed out from jetlag, we were exploring each other's bodies. Okay, okay, mainly it was *them* exploring *my* body, because Leander really had a thing for having me tied up, and Janus *really* liked the sadism of tying me in awkward positions that gave him access to my ass.

Except that Leander hadn't forgotten Janus's little trick the first time they'd both taken me at once—not listening and having me raw when Leander had clearly wanted that honor only for himself.

Janus's cock had strictly been suited up ever since.

But Leander had continued to fuck me no condom, even after I took the morning after pill. One day while the guys did press without me, I visited a women's clinic and came out with an oval pack of pills.

I don't know if conversations were had that day out of my hearing, but everything in front of me had become copacetic between the brothers. They were vibing with a harmony I hadn't seen from them before.

Janus sheathed up, and Leander dommed our scenes, and I came over and over and higher than I knew was possible. How had I not known what my own body could do? Good God! It was like I was meeting my body for the first time. And myself.

I was dirty. I was kinky.

I loved it when they called me their slut.

I wanted to be a whore. It made my clit pulse when they called me dirty things and talked about how hard they wanted to fuck me. I didn't even blush anymore when I talked about that—them *fucking me*. I begged them for it every night. And any afternoon we could steal back to the hotel.

I begged Janus to spank my naughty ass because of how amazing it felt when it jiggled the flesh of my butt and my pussy. I begged him to spank me harder, and then I regretted it, and then I blissed out on the pain because it bloomed into pleasure. A pleasure I never could have imagined.

I thought about the little church girl I'd been sometimes, and I thought about how my Daddies were defiling me now, and that made me come even harder when all three of them had their hands on me.

My father had always called women who dared show cleavage *whores* and shamed any woman he ever saw having a good time or smiling. Or doing anything other than living a life of obedience, depression, oppression, and misery.

So fuck yes, I was a *whore*. For my new Daddies. Daddies who *actually* took care of me. Who valued me, even if it was only in the explosive scenes and nights we shared, for *me*. Who called me beautiful and precious and worshiped my body. I first discovered what it was to orgasm, and then I discovered multi-orgasms, and sometimes, they made my body just continually shake in pulsing pleasure when I got into that weird, dreamy headspace only Janus and Leander taking me together could get me to...

"Where the fuck do you think you're going?" Leander reached out and grasped my thigh, pinching and making me yelp. I crawled back into bed instead of getting out, giving into what I knew he wanted.

"It's our last day in London. We've got to get going." I felt like I was glowing from within as I smiled at him. He was so beautiful in the morning. I mean, yes, he was beautiful all the time, but God, in the morning, he took my breath away.

It wasn't just his looks, which he obviously shared with Janus. It was in his eyes. In the morning, there was something more vulnerable, like he allowed me to see in a little deeper before all his masks went up.

His hand caressed down my hip to my ass. "There's always time to linger." He squeezed, then slid his hand further down my thigh, hiking my leg up over his hip and spreading me.

My breath hitched as I slid into him. He was hard. And we were both naked. With one slow thrust of his hips, he entered me.

I gasped and then breathed in, loving the wet slide of him. I was always drenched for them. If I was wearing panties, they were always soggy. And if not, then my tiny hairs, which my daddies insisted I keep, were forever damp little curls.

My fingers scratched against Leander's shoulder as he continued pressing in. The cone of him was so *thick*.

I whimpered and clutched his ass with my foot. "Oh, *Daddy*."

"Call me Leander." His voice was a deep rasp in the morning, and my eyes fluttered open. His eyes glowed silver in the morning light with little flecks of gold. I nodded, entranced by him.

"Leander," I breathed out, biting back the rest of what I wanted to say. Because as I gazed into the eyes of the man buried so deep inside me, staring into me with eyes that begged me to look straight into his soul, I knew that I was a goner. I loved him. I loved him, I loved him, I loved him.

I think I loved his brother too. I loved all of them, all of it. I'd loved every moment of the last two weeks.

Which was just fucking terrifying.

"Hope," Leander said, his hand lifting to push hair back from my face. He shifted his hips back and then thrust forward, again insanely slowly so that I felt every inch of him dragging against every inch of me. "Hope, these last two weeks have been—"

"Wakey wakey time," Milo said as he slammed open the door and stepped into the room.

I yelped and buried my face in Leander's chest.

"Jesus, Milo, can't you see I've got my dick deep in our woman here? What the fuck do you think you're doing busting in here like that?"

Milo shut the door behind him. "Well, I figured since y'all just finished fucking her three hours ago that you'd be full up for a little while longer!"

Janus popped his head up from behind Leander and slid a hand around to reach for me. "Huh? It's cocks up again?

Alright, flip her over so I can get at her too. Lemme just—Okay, okay, yeah, I'm ready."

"What?" Milo said. "No. It's time to get up. We've got places to be, places to be!" He clapped his hands loudly as he strode into the room. Meanwhile, Janus had gotten up on his knees over his brother to reach for me and Leander's fabulous cock kept fucking me.

I came with a high-pitched squeal. Far harder than was appropriate in the moment.

"Well, fuck," Milo said with a mock sigh. "Now I'll never get them moving."

22

SEGGZ ON THE BEACH

"I can't believe I let you talk me into this," I said, crossing my arms over my chest and taking several steps backwards. The vista before me was stunning. And terrifying.

The blue-black English Channel lay like a glinting sapphire below the cliff Milo had just driven us to.

I backed right into Leander's chest. His arms wound around me and he squeezed me to him. "Janus, Milo and I have done this before, Princess," Leander said. "It's safe or we wouldn't have brought you here."

"She's not jumping," Janus stated from behind us. "She just watches."

I felt Leander turn his head to look back at his brother. "Fuck off. She jumps if she wants to." Then his voice was in my ear. "And it's a high that really shouldn't be missed, baby. I want to show you the world and wake your body up to every thrill it can know. After we jump, we'll fuck while we ride the adrenaline high."

Leander spun me around so I was facing him and pulling me in, dipping his lips down to mine.

"No, you fucking won't," Janus said, stepping up and yanking Leander backwards by his shirt, which also jerked me forwards.

Leander steadied me, then turned and exploded at his brother, "What the fuck, bro? You almost knocked her on her ass."

"At least I'm not trying to throw her over a fucking cliff."

Leander rolled his eyes. "Don't be a sexist fuck off. Milo brought us to the low jump. It's not even twenty feet. A bunch of girls were here when we jumped last summer."

Leander held a hand out toward me, the same eyes that had looked into my soul this morning smiling out at me. Boyish and free. "Do you trust me?"

I grinned back at him, thrust my hand into his and squeezed as hard as I could. "Fuck yes, I do."

"Wait, no. Leander, I'm fucking serious—"

"Janus, chill out," Milo said. "They're just doing the small jump—"

"Let go of me, you fuck," Janus was saying, but that was the last thing I heard because Leander and I were running, straight out, right towards the edge of a cliff.

"Point your legs when you hit the water," Leander yelled.

And then we leapt out, out, out, right off over the cliff and into nothingness.

I didn't hesitate one bit.

With Leander by my side, I couldn't imagine not making the leap.

First, we were jumping. And then, oh God,— *We're falling, falling straight down!*

I screamed at the top of my lungs, losing Leander's hand as I waved them in frantic circles, screaming and screaming some more and kicking wildly and screami—

I *slammed* into the water and tumbled.

Water rushed in my mouth. Up my nose.

Swirled in my ears as I lurched end over end.

Which way was up?

I tried to kick with my legs, to get some control of my tumbling limbs. For a moment, I hung suspended in the darkness, water bubbles still swirling all around me, salt stinging my tongue and nose and eyes. I fought to keep them open anyway.

And saw that one area was lighter than the rest of the darkness. I swam towards it, transferring my momentum. My lungs burned and it registered that I'd been stupid, stupid—screaming had been stupid, I should have been *breathing* before I hit the damn water because what I wouldn't do now for a damn breath. Or even half a breath. I'd give a million bucks for even an extra hitch of air in my lungs as I swam harder towards the light.

Arms grabbed my shoulders and hauled me to the surface right when I thought I wouldn't make it.

I sucked in a huge, life-giving breath. And then another and another. Tears squeezed out of my eyes. And then I started laughing. I had a twin on either side of me and Milo swimming right in front of us, holding my hips.

I laughed and threw my head back, "Whoooooooop!" I screamed. I let out another feral whoop and then looked to Leander.

"Fuck me." I gripped his neck. "I feel the adrenaline j-j-j-just like you s-s-s-s-said!"

"Are you fucking kidding?" Leander said, sounding half hysterical, "We thought you were dead. We broke the surface and you weren't *there*. Hope, you weren't fucking there."

He clung to me, the boyish smile gone as he swam towards a sand bank below the cliff. Janus seemed on board with this plan because they were both swimming the same. Same strokes. Identical movements. We moved faster than I would've imagined through the water and then I was being hauled up on the beach.

My body had been through so many sensations and emotions in the last minute and a half, I could hardly tell up from down.

"You guys!" I slapped their shoulders. "That was amazing! Can we go again?"

"No!" both twins yelled in unison, then looked each other in the eye as they each yanked off the soaked shirts they're wearing.

Which I decided was swoon-worthy so I lay back on the sand as the sun set on our side of the cliff, casting warmth on us and light on my men.

"Enough with this little adventure," Janus growled. "It's time to get her somewhere warm."

"I know how you could make me warm," I said with a smile, fire still lighting my blood as I caressed a finger down Janus's arm.

He glared at me, or tried to, and then he shook his head. "That's it. Brat's gotta learn her lesson. I've counted so many infractions tonight, I've run out of fingers. Ignoring me and jumping off that goddamned cliff—"

"Leander was taking me with him!" I protested.

"*Talking back*." Leander said, helping Janus get me to my feet.

"Why?" I whined, holding out a hand towards the sunlight. "Why do we have to leave the sunshine?"

"Because, honey," Janus whispered, "look behind you."

"What?" I said, finally looking further back on the beach. I'd been so discombobulated when they first dragged me up on the beach, I hadn't exactly paused to take in the landscaping.

It turned out it wasn't just a shallow little area. The beach led to shallow caves beneath the cliffs. And far back in one of the caves a fire had already been lit by someone. Wow, Milo really had outdone himself setting all this up for us—chairs, robes, and blankets.

I felt giddy at the surprise. They'd surprised *me* this time. My heart went squishy.

"We could have just driven her down here," Janus muttered to Leander.

"I know." Leander said, shortly. "We'll talk later."

They'd talk later? So they *did* talk about me when I wasn't there? That wasn't fair. They didn't talk to me about each other. I wanted in.

"Here," Milo hurried ahead and pulled a fluffy robe off a pile, holding it out for me.

"Strip her," Leander ordered.

"Duh," Janus said.

And then I was being stripped by my two sexy daddies. I went limp, only holding myself up enough to stand. It felt amazing to give into their caring, firm hands as they peeled my cold, wet shirt up over my tummy, then over my breasts. Janus's rough fingertips skimmed over my nipples, turning them into hard, pebbled points.

It felt so good to let them fuss and undress me. To feel a pair of hands on each of my legs as they peeled off my jeans. Down went the jeans. Firm hands steadied me as I stepped out of the wet jeans. It was hard to get through the sticky, wet hole at the bottom, but they helped me finally get free of the damn things.

I was giggling by the end of it, but when Leander lifted me up in his arms, I gasped, fully immersed only in the feel of his cool chest against mine. I loved being held in his arms. He'd never carried me anywhere. No one had. I wasn't a small girl, but Leander carried me as if I were. I loved him even more for it. It wasn't far to the fire, but it still meant so much to me.

He set me smoothly down on my feet and Janus was again there at my side. The fire was warm on my front and the twins were cool at my back.

"Come get warm," I urged them both, trying to pull them around to my side so they could feel the firelight. "It's freezing out of the water. And the water is always freezing. Freaking England!" Still, I wouldn't have taken back that jump for anything in the world. I'd never felt so... so free of all I'd ever been told I was supposedly *allowed* to be. Every moment with the boys I'd been bucking free of it, finally, firmly, all the way.

I was finally my own.

And goddamn, it was fucking amazing. I wanted to dance on the fucking beach, it felt so freeing!

So I did.

One amazing man on either side of me, my hips began to move from side to side. Immediately, strong arms wrapped around me, and then Milo was behind me, his coolness slowly warming because our bodies were skin on skin as the twins moved to my sides just like I'd wanted.

"You all make me feel so safe. Safe enough to find myself for the first time."

"Who do you see?" Janus asked. "Because I know who I'm looking at."

I blushed and looked down, my hips still moving to the sultry salsa playing only in my head. Mikayla and I'd once gone to a salsa club in Austin and it was a *real* salsa joint with people who knew how to *really* dance—they even taught salsa lessons an hour before so newbies could learn. It was one hot night out where Mikayla actually got me to let loose. We had what we still both agree to this day was the best night of our lives.

So that was the music playing in my head as the sun set: a sultry, dark club, where I'd had the first taste of men touching me and moving with me sensually to a beat... Yeah, it was the best thing I'd ever felt before the twins had shown me this new world of possibilities.

Behind us, the sun began to set. Milo moved behind me, matching his hips to mine. He pulsed with me to the beat in my head. I couldn't tell if it was sweat or seawater dripping down my temple when I licked saltwater off my lips, which elicited a "fuuuuuuuck," from Janus.

"I need my cock in her," Janus said, reaching down towards my pussy and tickling the hairs there with his big fingers. "I'll fuck her good and hard. *Vigorous*. Friction will get her warmer faster."

"You think I can't do vigorous?" Leander bit out, hand joining his brother's from the other side of my body. Two hands on my pussy. I breathed out shakily, body trembling.

"I don't know," Janus said, grinning at his brother, a grin that had an edge. I swung my head around at Leander, almost afraid to see he'd take it as some sort of challenge.

"What you don't get, brother," Leander said, hand massaging my pussy deep with his whole hand. "It's that it's about the quality and command of the touch, not how fast you fuck." My whole body spasmed, rocking my pelvis forward, making my bellybutton clench with my orgasm, such pleasure, such pleasure, oh god, oh god, right up my sternum, how did they make me come so fast, so good, oh God, I was melting, I was light.

"Oh God, Daddy, I'm coming so hard," I hissed out, "you make me come so hard." I ground myself against Leander's hand.

"Fuck her," Leander ground out to Janus. "Fuck her now. Fast and hard. Fast as you can. Like you're a goddamn teenage boy jerking off in her cunt fast. And we'll see who makes her come harder."

I spun, turning my ass out so Janus had the best access to it, so wet I was sure it was dripping down my leg. I'd just come so hard I didn't know if I'd squirted, but if a woman didn't squirt during an orgasm that intense, I didn't know when she fucking *did.*

But Janus's strong hands came to my waist and he spun me roughly back to face him. "I want your cunt, I want you raw, and I want to look into the eyes of my goddamned woman while I fuck her."

And with that, he laid me down on a fluffy robe that someone had laid out close enough to the fire to be warm but not burned. And then he started *fucking* me. Like a battering ram. Actually, it was like Leander had done—but just those couple times when it felt like I'd been fucking the devil out of him. But now, it was Janus's turn. Janus's devil.

Right after I'd just come from one of the hardest, most adrenaline-fueled orgasms of my life, and having Janus fill me right at that moment, *oh*—

I started coming, muscles rippling all around his shaft—

"Fuck, guys," Janus ground out through his teeth. "She's coming around me already. She's fucking clenching so hard. This fucking angel is coming on my dick the goddamn second I get it inside her." He reached down underneath me, grabbed my ass, and angled me in such a way that he slid in another inch deeper. When I screamed, my orgasm amping higher at the new angle, he covered my mouth with his hand. I could still breath through my nose, but only just.

It was the hottest fucking thing, him fucking me and silencing me while he glared down at me like he'd never wanted anything more than to fuck the ever-loving shit out of me.

I sucked in a breath through my nose and gave in to him.

"She's the hottest fucking thing I've ever seen," Milo said from where he stood watching nearby. "My cock is so fucking hard. I won't let myself come yet. I won't let myself because you deserve more respect, baby. You deserve me to hold out as long as possible."

Oh God. Janus's cock was as thick as Leander's but he used it completely differently. He was a battering ram. He did exactly as Leander had commanded.

"Baby, I gotta fuck you warm," Janus whispered, and I giggled, at first thinking he was joking. But the way he lifted himself above me with hands on either side of my head and ground his hips against mine in a way that allowed him to thrust deep, quick, and with *exceptional* friction, I could only, oh, oh, oh— He was going faster, and harder— *harder*...!

Then Leander was bent at my other side. Leaning down, he pushed his brother's hand out of the way and kissed me. His lips were vigorous, and it was like I could feel the transfer of heat from him to me. He bowed over me, taking advantage of the ground his brother had given up, forcing Janus to lift one of his arms.

"Hey, asshole," Janus said, but Leander just kept kissing me.

"Oh yeah," Janus muttered, "well, it'll be my cock hitting her G-spot that's responsible for 'heating her up.' Oh, and when I hit her F. And her B sharp."

"My what?" I giggled between a gasp as Janus readjusted his position so that his very formidable cock did indeed bang a particularly lovely spot deep inside me with every one of his fast, furious *thrusts* that oh, oh wow, oh holy—holy—

"That," Janus said, breathing heavily as he continued to thrust in quick, steady bursts, "is your B sharp."

"Oh!" I said, or more like squealed. Because, oh dear Mary mother of God and all that's holy...!!! I... was... melting.

"That's fucking right, that's fucking right, little whore. Come around Janus's dick. Let him spread you. Your pink little cunt just split wide open for him. We can all hear you squelching around him. He's fucking ramming you and you're gushing for it. Goddamn. Look at him ram into you over and over like that. That's gotta hurt, baby. Does it hurt? Just a little? 'Cause I know you like it when it hurts. You can be a little pain slut, can't you?"

I squealed and thrust my hips feebly back at Janus.

"Look at our brother," Leander ordered, grabbing my face and turning me towards Milo. He stood beside us in the light of the fire as the sun set even further. Milo had his cock out, long and straight and pulsing furiously in his fist. He squeezed it beyond what it seemed like it could take as he looked me up and down. He made eye contact as he continued intimately, "We both like a little pain, don't we, baby. It's good to be a dirty little fucking slut. 'Cause then you get to get fucked like little sluts do."

"How do dirty little sluts get fucked?" Leander asked, playing with my hair while Janus fucked me even more furiously still.

"Dirty little sluts are cum buckets," Milo said, stepping closer as he jerked himself ruthlessly, squeezing the knob of his head harder even than he had his shaft. "After your brother stuffs her with his cum, then you gotta fuck her. 'Cause the little whore likes a train of dicks. She's gotta be stuffed."

I spasmed up against Leander as Milo kept up his dirty talk, and Leander bit my bottom lip, grabbing one of my nipples in between his forefinger and his thumb and *twisting*—

I howled into Leander's mouth.

Janus fucked me harder, positively sawing in and out of my pussy, grinding his groin on my swollen clit and labia while Leander kept twisting and twisting—

I screamed and spasmed against the twins.

"Look at our little slut," Milo said. "She can't get enough dick. She needs it. She wants to lick it. She wants dick in her mouth, doesn't she? If she had dick in her mouth, she'd be the perfect portrait."

I blinked and looked up at Leander. For once my hands weren't bound so I was free to reach up to him and caress his jaw. I nodded excitedly. I felt so much pleasure in this moment, and I could feel how much pleasure I was bringing Janus.

I wanted to complete the circle. I needed Leander in my mouth. I needed to taste his salty-bitter cum. I needed to swallow and suck and drive him so wild he couldn't wake in the morning without wanting my mouth around his cock, couldn't go to work or walk onto set without dreaming of my luscious lips swallowing him down to his balls—

I pulled back from him just far enough to plead, "Please. Daddy." And then, eye to eye, earnest with the man I'd made love to this morning and played with this afternoon, "*Leander*."

"Fuck." And then he whispered, "You know in the end I can never deny you anything."

Leander got to his knees and bent over me, angling his fat shaft down with his hand to my mouth.

I swallowed him eagerly, reaching up to take him with my hand. I'd always had petite hands and it thrilled me every time my little hand wouldn't fit around his big cock. So much so that I spasmed around his brother even as I swallowed Leander down.

"Godfuckingdammit," Leander swore.

He was salty. I licked him furiously with my tongue as I widened my mouth to swallow him deeper. And deeper still.

"Damn, baby," Milo said. "That's right. Mmmm, yes, honey. The way your flesh sucks around Janus's cock while he fucks you so good. But damn, I don't even know if it holds a candle to watching your sweet little slut mouth suck down Big Daddy's cock. Oh, he's going deep, isn't he? Oh, that's deep. Oh baby, he's going in your throat. He's choking you. Can you handle it, baby? Can you handle what Big Daddy's giving you? Can you handle this test?"

Tears squeezed out of my eyes as my throat bulged with Leander's cock. I looked up his torso at his face and there was something on it. Something I couldn't explain. An intensity and an anger and an intense, intense lust—

Our gazes locked. "You can take it, baby," Leander whispered. "Baby can take it." It was assurance as much as an order.

My pussy squelched around Janus and I nodded, determined. I'd survived the Channel. This I actually *wanted.* I remembered what it had been like to trust Leander and leap. I remembered what it was like in that magical space when I gave in to both boys fucking me simultaneously front and back. And I went loose. I gave myself over to Leander's command of me.

He felt it, I knew, because a smile and pride I'd never seen before came over his face. He didn't let up his cock on my throat. If anything, he fucked me deeper. "You can take it, baby. I know you can."

And just when I was sure I couldn't anymore, he pulled back and let me breathe again. And right after I'd caught my breath, his cock was pressing back at my lips. He was still salty from the sea and delicious, and I licked him, loving him as I gave in to his command of my body.

I imagined the picture Milo saw, me on the beach, laid out by the fire like a not-so-virginal sacrifice. Two men with huge, muscled backs looming over me. One ass pumping furiously as he fucked the living daylights out of me, while the other grasped my hair like I was a ragdoll and fucked my throat as if I were just that, a doll.

Fucking hell, I loved that image. I was Daddy's little doll and they'd brought me to the beach along with the rest of their luxury equipment, to fuck and service them. I experimented suctioning my mouth and throat around Leander's thick cock and humming low notes.

"Godfuckingdammit," Leander swore. "This sweet little bitch is deep-throating me like a trained fucking whore. Yes. Fuck. Yes. *Just like that*." He grabbed my hair low at the base of my head and fucked my face hard.

"Harder," Leander grunted out to his brother, and I could tell I had his tight control slipping, which I *loved*. I suckled and hummed and reached up to play with his balls, squeezing them up tight against his body in a way I'd noticed he liked.

He came like a freight train down my throat. And then pulled out suddenly so that hot, salty cum was spilling out over my lips and down my chin. And then Milo was striding forward and crouching on his knees opposite Leander—Janus still vigorously fucking me this entire time.

"And now I get to add my cum to these tits, which I fucking love," Milo said. "You don't know it but all the time I'm sneaking peeks at your chest. I'm fucking obsessed with your nipples. And you're always getting hard little nipple peaks. Sometimes I can barely get any work done for staring at your nipples."

I lost my breath. Milo was usually so mild-mannered. He was the serious, calm one of the bunch. And respectful. He never gave any clue as to this filthy secret thought-life he lived.

And now to hear it so exposed—this was the first time he'd really truly let me see this side of himself. He'd only observed quietly before.

He squeezed his cock hard, rough and fast, slapping the knob of his cock against my breasts. "Oh, these fat, fat titties. I dream about them. I *daydream* about these perfect little nipples. All I want to do is watch my brothers fuck you and then come on these fine-as-fuck titties."

He reached down with the hand not on his cock to pluck at my nipples. It made them stiffen into tight, hard peaks.

I squealed and squirmed, still trying to swallow down Leander's load of cum, while also trying to get ahold of this new reality of Milo's commanding dirty talk. It was so hot. Fresh wetness sprung to lubricate Janus's way.

"And now Janus gets to unload on you," Milo said, "and if you didn't notice, Leander allowed him to go raw. Have you watched the ecstasy on brother Janus's face?"

I looked down, and then up, and really got a look at Janus... and damn, Milo was right. I hadn't realized. Leander hadn't made Janus wear a condom, and I doubted it was an oversight. He'd let him have me raw.

But then Leander had still butted in and overshadowed Janus, who had been there steadily working me in the background the entire time. Was it a rivalry thing between them? Or just a natural outpouring of their testosterone trying to lay claim on me?

Either way, looking at Janus now, I was determined to give to him at least as much or more as I'd just given to Leander. He'd been patient, and kind, and had really only been looking out for my safety up on the cliff ledge when he hadn't wanted me to jump. It had been scarier than I'd anticipated and while I wouldn't take it back, I appreciated the instinct to protect. It meant a lot.

I clenched all my Kegel muscles around him, or whatever the hell you called those muscles down there. Anyway, I *clenched.*

I clenched and I rolled. When I really focused in on my center, I could feel the very tip of his knob deep inside me. He'd moved on to short, intimate thrusts. He was leaning into B sharp again. Oh damn, this man.

Janus leaned down, reaching up and shoving Milo out of the way.

Janus looked me in the eye for one blink, two, and then he kissed me. Kissed me deep and sweet, and fucked me slow and deep, and my pussy that had been so desensitized by all the fucking, and yet *super*sensitized at the same time—

Janus ground his hips down and into me as his cock thrust in—

I wrapped both arms around his neck and clenched him to me.

"Tell me you love me," Janus whispered into my ear so that only I could hear.

I blinked in surprise but looked up at the man who was undeniably not just fucking me, but *making love* to me...

"I-I-I," I stuttered, and then I told him the truth, "I love you."

A grin like sunlight after a storm broke out over Janus's face as he pulled me to him, thrust deep, and came inside me. "I love you too."

I felt a rush of joy along with the rush of Janus's cum.

...and then I glanced over Janus's shoulder at Leander, who looked positively, absolutely, beyond pissed.

23

FEASTING IN DUBAI

Our trip to Dubai was far less eventful than the one to London had been. No private jet, for one. Just first class on Emirates, a top-of-the-line airline.

The flight attendants were exceedingly professional in giving us our space and some semblance of privacy in our four-seat pod, facing each other. The other passengers, however... Well, the twins were quite large and quite recognizable, and they were clocked within two seconds of walking into the gate area. So unfortunately, a brunette kept butting into our little pod to talk Janus's ear off half the flight, in something between fangirling and an attempt at flirting?

So, no hanky panky. Leave it to the twins to convince me otherwise sometime—but I'd consider my mile high club badge earned already and call it a day. Turbulence during climax had been an exciting but entirely unnerving experience, lemme tell ya.

But back to Dubai! Oh my God, this city! It was my first time here. In all my crisscrossing the world while being a publicist for Destiny and Mikayla, we'd always somehow passed over Dubai. The closest I'd been was Cairo.

And that was… nothing like this.

I'd never seen *anything* like this, to be honest. I clutched Milo's hand as we navigated down a beautifully tiled sidewalk, buildings lit up to the sky on either side of us. Janus was in front of us leading, while Leander flanked behind.

There was a Michelin star restaurant within walking distance of the hotel. The boys thought Leander should be unknown enough here, in spite of the little incident on the plane. The brunette had been British, anyway. Even Milo agreed that with a little disguise, walking around on the street should be safe enough. If you could call hats and sunglasses *disguises*. Janus did put on a fake mustache too. More because I think he got a kick out of the damn thing, but it did help them look a *little* less like twins. It was their identical build that was impossible to disguise, though.

According to Leander, what was life without a little thrill?

As we walked the gorgeous streets of Dubai, *every* part of the city looking like the richest and most expensive part of any big, metropolitan city, I could only look around open-mouthed.

"This place is insane," I said, gaping up at the neon lights and buildings that made the night look like day. We'd just passed out of sight of the sea with its turquoise waters, lapping almost at the edge of the monstrously tall buildings, it seemed. We'd stopped to watch the sun set. It was impossibly beautiful. The buildings appeared to simply sprout out of nowhere between the desert and the sea. Really, it seemed an impossible place all around, for a thousand reasons.

"Welcome to the city that *truly* never sleeps," Janus said with a grin.

Even Leander smirked, and he usually only liked being out of the house if he was hurling himself off something high and terrifying or racing at inhuman speeds.

Oh dear, what had I just gotten myself into, accepting a night out on the town with them?

Especially when we hadn't even slept yet? I mean sure, we'd all gotten a few hours here and there on the seven-hour flight from London.

It was ten o clock by the time we'd gotten checked in at the hotel, and apparently that was when nightlife in Dubai *started.*

And here we were. And to be honest, I was starving. The spiced bean curd and peppers had been delicious, just a too-small, fancy little first class airplane portion.

So yeah, I could eat. In fact, I was in the mood for dessert. Like, all I wanted to do was stick my face in the dessert tray—I was getting *that* kinda hungry.

"Where exactly is this amazing restaurant supposed to be?" I asked, looking around.

"Hold on," Janus said, pausing in front of us and looking down at his phone. "I swear it's supposed to be, like..." A furrow deepened in his brow as he frowned at the little screen. "Dammit, we were just on top of it, but now we passed it by or something?" He swung his head around to look back towards the corner we'd just passed. "Did you see a sign that said, well, dammit, now I can't find it—" He was fumbling with his phone, thumbing between apps.

Milo swore. "You said you knew where this place was. You said you'd been there *before*."

"We have, we have," Janus said. "It's just been a while."

"Give me the phone," Leander said, reaching past me and Milo to yank the phone out of his brother's hand.

"Hey—" Janus protested but the phone was already gone.

"It's right up ahead," Leander said after a quick glance at the phone. He shook his head like it was the most obvious thing in the world. "Across the street."

Janus shook his head. "It's not. I looked."

"Diagonally. *There.*" Leander pointed.

"Fine." Janus said. Sounding annoyed. Glaring at his brother.

"Yay, we found it." I wanted to put my arms around them both to soothe any friction, but that would likely only draw unwanted notice to us. Instead, Milo broke the tension by grabbing my hand again and hauling me across one street after the walk light turned, and then the next. Leander jogged after us, then Janus, too.

There it was. *Torno Subito.*

One of the best Italian places in the world outside of Italy, smack dab in the middle of a desert. Because the best chefs from around the world came to this oasis to cater to the rich and famous. And as we passed through the glass doors into the brightly lit, colorful open space, a sign hung that said, *Eating is Emotion*.

And I thought, with a grin deep in the loins of my heart: this is my kind of place.

I ORDERED GLAZED wagyu flank steak with cacao sauce. Because mama didn't raise no fool. But as delicious as it was, as much as the meat *melted* in my mouth, I didn't finish it all.

Because I knew that while I *had* to try their tiramisu, how could I not, how could I *not* see what their sweet pizza with dark chocolate, hazelnut, and black truffle tasted like? How, I ask you? *How?*

I couldn't not. And Leander, Janus, and Milo agreed. Finally, something everyone agreed on. Which was good because during everyone's salads it had been tense, and I'd been miffed, since this restaurant was too amazing an experience to ruin on pissy emotions.

So I played footsie with both twins until Milo whispered that I had to knock it off, this was not the country for that. Instead, I just ate my bread in a seductive manner. I'd dip my finger in the seasoned oil provided, and then rub it all along the long, thin cut slices of bread they served before dinner.

That improved everyone's moods perceptibly. Or at least distracted them from each other by focusing them on me until dinner was served.

I noticed that while only Milo also ordered dessert, the twins seemed quite engaged with watching me devour every bite of mine. They seemed to especially enjoy when I licked my spoon clean. With the tiramisu, well, there was a lot of spoon licking. And it turned out the same was true of the chocolate pizza, because those little chocolate truffle bits were *especially clingy*, and I really had to work them with my tongue—

"All right," Janus said, his fist hitting the table so hard as he stood up that several people at the table nearest ours looked our way. Milo waved at them and mouthed, *sorry*, then looked back at our group.

"I've got to go fucking dancing now," Janus leaned in and whispered. "Let's get to the clubs where grinding is allowed."

Leander allowed a smirk at his obviously horny brother. "Why do you think I told Milo to book the hotel I did? The hotel, the clubs, they're all right here."

I was shocked. "But you—" I stared at Leander. "You never party."

He shrugged. "People know me in New York. It's exhausting."

"What about London?"

"I used to be able to, there. These days." He shook his head. "Not so much. But here," he smiled and breathed in deep. "To people here I'm just one more rich prick from the West with money to blow."

I arched an eyebrow and laughed. Leander just kept breathing in deep till his chest was filled, then he finally exhaled. All I could smell was amazing food and lots of perfume and cologne. But Leander did look more relaxed.

I guess I hadn't realized how much it got to him, always being examined like a bug under a microscope back home, or even London. He never got a break from it, huh? Except when he came someplace far, far away like this.

I was suddenly determined to make this night good for him. No wonder he'd been so amped up getting off the plane.

I dared run a hand up Leander's thigh and giving his cock a quick squeeze through his slacks before darting it away again, all underneath the table.

"Sounds like fun." I winked at him, thrilling in the way his eyes and nostrils flared at me.

"Oh baby, we're going to have fun playing tonight." His voice was low, dangerous like it got when we were playing. "On the dance floor and off."

24

TWIN TANGO

After dinner we hit *Cavalli Club Dubai.*

It was the second-best club in the entire *world.* At least according to the very sophisticated ranking it had been awarded by *Luxury Magazine.*

These were the things you learned in my business, because it was better not to just show up at the door and trust they knew who you were. I'd called ahead at all the top clubs to let them know we'd be in town and might be visiting anytime in the next two weeks.

After a check of our ID's, the bouncer let us cut in through the front of the long line to get in. Some people pulled out phones and pointed them Leander's way, but it was nothing to New York and no one even came up and asked him for an autograph. It felt amazing to walk around so freely.

Then, as soon as we stepped inside, my jaw dropped. Could this night get any better?

I gripped Milo's hand. The floor was black marble and the walls sparkled. "The walls are so—"

"They're Swarovski crystals." Leander leaned over as he relieved me of my wrap and handed it over to a concierge who had suddenly appeared to check our coats and bags. I handed off my purse as well. "There's over three-hundred and fifty-thousand of them studded in the walls all over the club. They spared no expense on the place."

The room was huge and dark, with lots of nooks and crannies. Along one wall a stage was lifted, with a tattooed DJ spinning. He was a whir of motion, sampling from different albums in a way that had the crowd buzzing with electricity. He created a sultry sound that had a bass thudding underneath our feet like a heartbeat.

"Someone owes me a dance," Janus said, snatching my hand from Milo's and pulling me onto the dance floor. He urged me close to him and yes, well, ahem... he hadn't exactly dealt with the problem I'd created earlier while teasing him with my sumptuous desserts. He was stiff and growing stiffer the more he—

I gasped as he spun me so that my ass was right against his almost fully hardened cock. His hand splayed across my tummy as he pulled me against him, and it made my sex clench at the memory of him inside me on the beach.

"We haven't had a chance to talk," he whispered in my ear. He drew my hair back from my neck. "About the things we said to each other. But I meant what I said, baby. I love you. I'm in this for real. Not just for a job, or a convenient fuck. I want you for *you*."

I blinked, unprepared for the assault of emotions his words brought. Though maybe I shouldn't have been. Because I should have prepared myself for this, for what I'd say whenever he and I *did* get time alone. My emotions were all so spun up when it came to these boys.

But with Janus so firm behind me, his commanding hands on my body, those hands that knew how to bring me such exquisite pleasure out of even more exquisite pain... the likes of which I'd bet we'd only *begun* to explore... my brain just spun and spun on a faster hamster wheel.

Out of all the boys, he'd always been the quickest to vulnerability, to pursue me, to be honest about what he was pursuing.

Was it really me he wanted, though? Or was this all about some rivalry that had existed long before me and would be there long after I was gone? Was I just some... playing field for their games? I cringed.

I spun to look over my shoulder, praying I'd find an answer in Janus's eyes. But his head was dipped down, and then I felt his lips on my neck. It tickled because of his fake mustache, making me giggle. He looked up and our eyes caught. My heart seemed to hiccup in my chest.

How could I deny what I felt for this man? His hands were suddenly at my waist. Then I was spinning again so that I was facing him. He leaned into me with the beat of the music, his hips notching neatly against mine so that again I felt him hard where I was soft.

He always made me feel so small and womanly.

And then he moved me to the music. I went liquid to his firm, commanding lead.

It was so sensual. His grip at my hip, the other arm around my back. The fancy club, the foreign locale, all of it dropped away in the embrace of Janus Mavros.

His eyes searched mine, and then his grip whipped me close so that we were pelvis to pelvis again. "Tell me," he demanded. "Did you mean it? When you said you loved me?"

I started to confess the truth in spite of the consequences. Whether he and his brother were playing games or not. "Janus, I've felt so con—"

"May I cut in?" Leander asked, suddenly appearing at our sides out of nowhere. But then, I supposed Janus had sucked me into a bubble apart from the world. I was so befuddled at Leander's sudden appearance, though, that I let go of Janus's neck.

Which Leander took as permission to whisk me away from Janus, deeper into the crowd.

"Wha— Leander! I was dancing with your brother!"

Leander didn't say anything for several long beats. He didn't thrust our pelvises against one another like his brother had. No, instead, he gently grasped both of my hands in his, then made his arms into a frame close to his body, drawing me near.

"Everything's been so busy lately. We haven't had the time alone I've wanted."

I glared up at him even as my body responded to his closeness and command. My feet fell into step with his without me even thinking about it. It was like... well, it was like fucking. We weren't doing fancy dance steps or anything, just moving back and forth. But it had some rhythm to it that I'd screw up if I thought about it too much.

So there was nothing to do but lean into Leander and abandon myself to it. "Janus and I were trying to have a conversation too. Look, I don't know how this is all supposed to work yet, but maybe instead of each of you trying to corner me, we could all talk together out in the open?"

"What did Janus want to talk to you about alone?" Leander asked, and I didn't like the edge to his voice.

I pulled back from him, interrupting our flow. "Are you *ordering* me to tell you? Am I not allowed private moments?"

His jaw flexed and he yanked off his sunglasses, which had looked ridiculous in the dark club, though plenty of other rich assholes around the place were wearing them too.

"I don't think you quite understand what's going on here,"

Leander said, his voice so low and deep it was barely audible over the music.

I got right up in his face. "Then why don't you explain it to me? Because I'm tired of feeling like a piece of meat in a tug of war between you and your brother."

Leander stepped back, a furrow in his brow like he was confused. "What are you talking about?"

I blinked at him. What the hell did he mean, *what was I talking about?*

Suddenly, all this globe-trotting and the second round of jet lag was hitting me. I waved a hand at him, no longer in the mood to try to unwind the Gordian knot that was the Mavros twins.

"I have to go to the bathroom." I started stomping off through the crowd.

Leander yelled my name but it was lost in the pounding beat of a new song the DJ was laying down. And this was one instance where Leander being such a giant was a hindrance. I was curvy and unassuming. I could squeeze through a crowd invisibly. He was a mountain in a bad disguise, theoretically trying to stay under the radar.

I only started looking for bathroom signs when I was about halfway across the huge dance floor. I glimpsed one in the direction I'd been headed. With a club this fancy, there were probably twenty bathrooms anyway.

I pushed through the golden-gilded black door into the bathroom, which was done in whites and golds.

There was a beautiful sitting area that looked like the parlors in the fanciest mansions Makayla and Destiny had ever partied in. I hurried through to the bank of mirrors and sinks. Each mirror was lined with lightbulbs and gold accents. It was officially the most glamorous bathroom I'd ever been in.

And all I could do was stare at myself in the mirror and

feel torn apart inside. I didn't look great. My lipstick was almost worn off from dinner. Dammit, why had I given my clutch to the door attendant? I needed to reapply. Though even if I'd had the bag, my mascara was getting smudged at the edges and I didn't have any handy repair for that—

Then I breathed out heavily and closed my eyes. *Jesus, just be honest with yourself, Hope.* The problem wasn't my frizzy-ass hair that didn't know what to do with this salty sea desert air.

It was time to ask myself the real questions. Even if they made me nauseous. My stomach swooped and not in a good way as I looked myself in the mirror and let the nasty voice in my head rip.

What was I really doing here, playing sex kitten to rich movie stars? Pretending I was living some teenage fantasy? All I could hear on repeat was Janus saying those things to me out on that dance floor, looking at me like I was his world.

... But he and his brother have been actors since they were children. I knew their secret now too—Janus was just as good of an actor as his brother. He used his talents differently, yes, but he was just as good.

And to be honest, while I wasn't the nice little religious girl I'd once been, I was still young. And impressionable, I had to admit it.

They'd bowled me over. Hook, line, and sinker.

And the reason I'd been so afraid to tell Janus the truth? I *was* in love with him. I was in love with Leander. *Hard.* And I was in love with Milo, my friendly confidant helping me organize travel and bookings... until he turned into the dirtiest talking stranger who would look but not touch...

I wished I wasn't wearing so much mascara. If I could just splash my face with some water. I fanned myself.

God, you'd think with such a fancy place, they could afford to crank up the AC. And then I frowned and put a hand to my forehead. It was damp, and all of a sudden I didn't feel so good.

Maybe dancing so soon after eating all that food hadn't been such a good idea.

Oh. My stomach lurched suddenly and I got a sick feeling at the back of my throat. Oh no!

I turned and ran for one of the toilets hidden behind a ten-foot tall pearlescent-white door. Just in time to empty the most amazing meal of my life into the gorgeous porcelain toilet of the second fanciest club in the world.

Hashtag winning.

I leaned an arm on the toilet lid and groaned while I reached for the toilet paper to swipe at my mouth.

"Oh, honey, are you alright?"

I tossed the paper into the bowl and flushed. I stood upright and looked behind me at a beautiful woman I hadn't even heard come in the bathroom. She was watching me, concerned. I was shaky on my heels but felt a little better. Though still queasy.

This night sure had taken a turn. "I-I'm fine," I said, reaching out for the stall frame to steady myself.

"You sure?" she said, grabbing a warm towel from a steamer box and handing it to me as if she didn't know what else to do. "Here. You look a little pale."

I took the towel, so soft and warm, and swiped at my face self-consciously. "Sorry, I—" I gestured behind myself. "This isn't like me. We just had a big dinner out and—"

"Look, it's not a big deal but, um..." She glanced nervously over her shoulder towards the door even though we were clearly the only two in the bathroom.

"What?" I asked as I finished swiping the cold sweat from my face. God, there was little I hated more than throwing up. It just made me feel awful all over.

The woman in front of me had thick, beautifully shaped eyebrows, especially highlighted as she leaned in towards me and one hiked up. "Look, you seem nice. And Lena's a bitch."

I jerked backward at hearing the name. This chick knew Lena? Did that mean Lena was here? In the club?

I looked towards the door just like the woman had.

"I won't tell her about anything I saw here." She waved a hand at my sudden obvious anxiety. "But you should know she sent me in here to spy on you and then make some heavy hints about how it was a bad look to be hanging on both Mavros brothers at once. How it would give people the wrong idea."

Shit. My back stiffened. "The wrong idea?"

The woman rolled her beautiful brown eyes. "Oh you know, all that bullshit with their last publicist. It's clear you guys are just out having fun. But Lena loves to stir up drama wherever she goes."

I wondered why she stayed "friends" with Lena, but there was more pressing information on the table.

"What the hell?" I said, lifting a hand to my forehead. I felt dizzy. I couldn't deal with Lena drama right now. We should've suspected she'd be here tonight. We knew she'd be in town and of course she'd come to this club since it was the best. Only the *best* for precious *Lena*.

And now she'd gone and seen us all unguarded around each other. But what had she really seen? The boys on just another adrenaline high adventure. Testing how far they could take things, not just in public, but in public here.

God! No wonder I'd gotten sick. My head was just catching up to what my body had obviously instinctively sensed about the situation. This whole thing was rotten.

"And fyi, the other reason she sent me in here was to distract you while she makes a move on Leander. I thought I'd give you a heads up. Seems like you're having a rough enough night."

I looked at her, touched by her random act of kindness. "Thanks. I didn't even get your name."

"Dakota," she said, then gave me a significant look, magnificent eyebrows in full effect. "But you didn't hear any of this from me. I gotta head out. You okay now?"

I nodded. "Thanks again."

She gave a little wave with her fingers and then pulled the door open.

I yanked my phone out to dial Milo. I officially needed him to get me out of here ASAP. I didn't need to see the Lena and Leander make-out session Part Deux as another publicity stunt.

But instead of the messenger app, I accidentally thumbed on the calendar app and it gave me the month view. Before I could click out of it, I stopped and paused. Every day was stuffed full of events.

There was something missing, though. The little discrete dots I put on the day my period started. It was a little trick I'd begun to track my periods when I'd had some weird inter-period spotting a few years ago.

But... there weren't any dots.

And I'd just thrown up.

I laughed out loud at how ridiculous the possibility was.

Then the laughter cut off sharply as I did some quick math. I'd first had sex with the twins on the plane to London... three weeks ago. We'd trusted the "day after" pill but had pushed the days because Leander had liked having me bare...

My thoughts were spinning too fast.

I wanted to deny it was possible. But three weeks after impregnation counted as *five* weeks pregnant. Information I only knew because of a pregnancy scare with Makayla last year.

And then I blinked. Thinking of Mak, I'd forgotten all about the little box o' goodies I'd thrown in my suitcase for the condoms I knew were in it. They were leftover from being on set with her last year. I'd just kept the little bag stowed in my luggage since the guys always had condoms on hand. I figured it was better than trusting year-old condoms anyway.

Now that I thought about it in my hour of need, though, there weren't just condoms in that little goody bag. After Mak's pregnancy scare, I'd also slipped a couple discreet pregnancy tests in. Mak traveled the world regularly and they could be extremely awkward to get in certain places. I hadn't thought to pull the tests out when I'd thrown the goody bag in my suitcase—considering I'd barely been able to admit to myself what I'd been hoping for when I'd added it in the first place.

Jesus, and now was I actually considering that I might be... by a *Mavros twin*???

No. No no no. No, the universe wasn't that cruel. Was it?

I started striding towards the door. But right as I was about to yank on the handle, I stopped and put a hand on my belly. And imagined a little being swimming around in there.

Holy shit. I stood there stunned.

Because what if?

What if I *was* pregnant?

25

ALL THREE NOW

Milo helped me out of the club, and then guided me down the sidewalk back towards the hotel.

He wrapped his arm around my back to protect me, even though for once, there weren't paparazzi hounding us.

I looked up into Milo's brown eyes and wondered why I had never appreciated him more. The twins were always spinning my head around, but it was Milo who was always there for me, steady, and never asking for more. Milo who was just as passionate as Leander and Janus, but who had more control than either, it seemed. And he wasn't playing games with me.

If anyone wanted me just for me, it was Milo.

I hugged his arm harder than was probably necessary, but it was reassuring to feel his strong muscles under my hands. The streets of Dubai were getting more crowded as the revelers came out to party. Leander hadn't been kidding when he said that nightlife started at ten o'clock around here.

"Are you okay?" Milo asked, as he helped me cross the street.

"I'm fine," I assured him. "I just needed to get out of there."

"I'll text the guys," Milo said, but I shook my head.

"No, I don't wanna cramp their style. Let's leave them be."

"But," Milo started, and I shut him down. "I've got a headache. Can we just go and let them know we're heading home?"

"Whatever you want, babe," he said, though I could see the concern in his eyes.

Thankfully, Milo took care of texting the guys so I could just focus on walking and forgetting the night. I'd deal with life tomorrow.

At least, that was what I thought.

Until we got the few blocks home to the hotel, and... the twins were there waiting for us in the lobby. Good Lord, had they taken a cab back just so they could beat us here?

"What the hell, Hope?" Leander strode toward us, looking furious. "Did you really think you could just ditch us?"

And I realized my mistake. Daddy wasn't happy. But I still didn't think that I had the bandwidth to deal with him or Janus.

Milo put out a hand. "She's tired. I told you, she has a headache."

"Why didn't *you* tell us?" Janus bypassed Milo to ask me. "When we were on the dance floor, you just took off? That's not cool."

And all of a sudden, I felt like bursting into tears. Which I just could not do in front of all of them. So I fled. Real mature of me, I know.

And of course, they were on my heels. As if I could outrun three hulking giants with huge leg strides.

They caught up to me by the time I made it to the elevator, and then they all crowded inside with me.

Three huge beasts of men and one tiny little me.

Of course, Leander immediately got right up in my space.

His body was flush against mine as he levered me against the wall.

"Enough, little girl. Enough evading. Enough running away. You have a headache, fine. We take care of you when you're hurting. But you never, *ever* run."

A thousand emotions cartwheeled through me. I wanted to yell at him that if that was true, then why did *he* keep hurting me? I didn't have a headache, I had a *heart*ache, and he and his brother were the ones doing it to me.

I wanted to scream at him and find out once and for all if this was just a game to them or not. But in spite of all the things I'd done with them over the past few weeks, all the courage I'd mustered to try things I never thought I'd do... I just couldn't get the words out.

I couldn't bear to find out if it was true. What if they *were* just playing with me?

Either they'd lie, and I'd be that much more devastated when it all came out. Or they'd tell the truth—that yes, it was a game—and it would all be over. How could either of those things be what I wanted?

So I kept my mouth shut and looked up into Leander's ever-changeable eyes. Then I whispered the only truth I could, "Please," I said. "Can we stop thinking for tonight? Can we all just go up to the bedroom and please stop thinking? Can you just make me *feel*? I want to feel all of your arms around me. Please." And then I added the word I knew would do him in: "Please, Daddy?"

It had the hoped-for effect. Leander's lips landed on mine, and then Janus was there too, his body warm. As Leander kissed me deeper, for once I couldn't care if it was because of the rivalry between them.

In this moment, with Leander's lips on mine, and three

pairs of hands wandering over my body as the elevator lift made my tummy swoop, did I care?

No, no I did not care.

I gave myself up to their touch. And it started getting heated.

At least until the elevator pinged and we all sprang apart. Not in time for the elderly couple not to catch an eyeful though.

I giggled as Leander grabbed my hand in his firm grasp and tugged me past the gaping couple and down the hall towards our room.

My feet felt light as air, like I was flying. Of course, with the men flanking me on all sides, their hands all but lifting me, I might as well have been.

Janus had the door key out and then we were inside.

Leander wasted no time. He had my dress up and over my head before I'd even had a chance to take in the room. We'd only had our luggage sent up earlier, the boys were in such a hurry to take me out on the town.

Of course, the suite was top of the line, dripping in luxury, in shades of golds and creams. Though he'd let go of my hand for a moment, while he helped me in the door, Janus took advantage and lifted me off my feet and carried me to the bed.

I was in nothing but my lingerie at this point.

How had this night flipped so quickly? I'd left the club determined to get some alone time and clear my head. Then again, this was so often how it went with them. I might have my own agenda, but they were always the ones in control.

Milo was the only one who stayed back, a furrow in his brow. I reached out a hand towards him. He still felt like my anchor in the storm.

With all of them here like this, there was no way to sneak

off and take the pregnancy test hidden in my luggage. But even at the thought, my brain blanked out.

Nope, couldn't handle thinking about. Maybe that was why I was so eager to give into them tonight. Giving in meant no more thinking or stressing or worrying about what may or may not be in my belly.

I wanted a few more hours of being irresponsible and giving in to all the things they could make me feel without considering any consequences.

Milo approached and when he got close enough, I clung to his hand. "Please," I begged. "I need you too, tonight."

His eyes widened, but he nodded. I noticed Janus and Leander exchange a glance, but they didn't say anything contrary to my request.

"Okay, baby," Leander said, crawling up on the bed beside me, stripping off his shirt as he came. He was frowning at me like I was a puzzle he was trying to figure out. "We do it your way tonight."

His hand came to my throat and he squeezed, not enough that I couldn't breathe but enough that I definitely felt it. "But that doesn't mean you don't have to do what Daddy says."

A gush of pleasure flooded my sex at his show of dominance and I thrust my neck harder against his grip, nodding furiously.

"Yes, Daddy," I hissed. Yes, I wanted to lose myself in play, in debauchery, in all of our bodies entwining.

Leander's pupils dilated as Janus tugged my panties down my thighs.

"Milo," Leander said, his jaw tight, "get your pants off and get your dick in our woman. You're feeling her sweet pussy around you tonight."

Milo groaned and when I looked at his face... He was looking down at me, naked and writhing between the two brothers, and I could see his lust clear as day. His hand was on his cock through his pants. But he was hesitating, even though he looked tormented by doing so.

"Milo," I said, reaching out for him again, meeting his tortured eyes. "Please, I want to feel you inside me. I'll squeeze you like your fist does. I'll squeeze you with all my muscles."

"Oh, Jesus," Milo swore and then he was on the bed with the brothers, crawling up from the bottom while Janus and Leander flipped me on my back and they spread my legs for him. He shoved his pants down in one motion, and then his cock was in his hand. He pumped it hard, and then lined it up.

He hesitated, his long, throbbing dick right at my lips.

I looked down my body. Janus and Leander were still holding my arms and legs on either side of me, spreading me wide. And there was Milo at my center, fist on his cock, his thighs shaking.

"You're so..."

I waited for him to say something filthy, for his dirty mouth to turn on. But instead he finished, "You're so fucking beautiful," he said, and then, fist still around the head of his cock, he rubbed his tip against my wet petals.

I groaned at the sweet friction. And then bucked my hips up against him involuntarily.

"You've got our little slut in heat for you," said Leander. "Show us how you play with her. Show us what a different cock feels like while Daddy Leander plays with her ass."

Milo started pushing in, and he was so slow with his thrust, it felt so—

Leander leaned over towards my ear. "Because we're taking all three of your holes at once tonight, baby. I haven't had your ass yet, and I'm fucking hungry for it."

"Janus," Leander snapped. "Deep throat her. Now. We're

going to use our little fuck toy up tonight. We're going to show her what happens when she runs away from us."

"Yes, Daddy," I said through his fingers still gripping my throat. "Fuck me. Fuck me everywhere."

"Stop dicking around and fuck her," Leander snapped at Milo. Milo's cock lurched the last of the way into me, and I moaned into Leander's hand on my throat.

"You like that, don't you," Leander said, his face coming within an inch of mine. "You love to feel him fuck you. You love to hear his balls slapping your ass."

And I did. That was exactly what I could hear. A rhythmic slap, slap, slap as Milo got into fucking me. I looked up at his face and he was looking down at where we were joined, his features astonished. He hiked one of my legs up in the air and started kissing the arch of my foot, fucking me even deeper at the new angle.

"Love seeing my cock disappear in you," Milo murmured, sounding drunk. "Gonna get lost in this pussy." And then his eyes closed and his head fell back. "Haven't felt pussy in forever. Jesus fuck, you feel so good."

He started fucking me hard and fast then.

And I wondered just how long it had been since he'd had sex like this. Actual sex with a woman instead of just watching.

"Janus," Leander snapped. "Her mouth. Deep. I mean it."

The bed shifted and then Leander was at my face and Milo groaned. "Oh fuck, oh fuck, oh fuck oh fuck."

I opened wide for Janus. It was his first time in my mouth. Leander reached underneath and pinched my ass. Hard.

"Down her throat. Stuff it down," Leander ordered. "Don't take it easy on her."

"Wider, baby," Janus said, hand on his cock, feeding himself into my mouth. I opened wider but Janus didn't shove inside like Leander said. He just ran the tip of his cock around my lips, like he was painting me with lipstick. And I guess he was, since there was precum on his tip, and he left salty traces of it all over my lips.

And then he pushed gently inside, popping the head through the ring of my lips. I licked up his slit, then round and round before suckling him.

"I'll just take it doubly as hard on her ass," Leander snapped, seeing Janus take it easy on me. "But she's taking all of us at once one way or another. Get our little slut over to the fucking couch. Sit her on her goddamn throne, impaled on her king where she fucking belongs."

And then all the sensation was gone—Janus from my mouth and Milo from my pussy, and hands were on me again. I could get so lost in these sessions with them. Leander would order the boys and I'd be dragged around like a ragdoll as they wrung all sorts of pleasures from me.

When I was right-side up again, I saw that Janus and Milo were carrying me towards a couch across the suite from the bed.

And Leander was already sitting there. Naked. His cock pointed straight up. Ready for me.

"You love your daddy's cock?" Leander asked, and his eyes were dark.

"I worship my daddy's cock," I breathed out.

Janus spanked my ass hard and I whimpered.

"Again," Leander ordered and Janus spanked me again. And again and again.

I felt my wetness leaking down my leg.

"Then sit down on your throne," Leander said. He spat in his palm and rubbed it up and down his huge cock.

And I knew how he meant for me to sit. Leander wanted my ass.

Janus and Milo had positioned me so I'd be sitting on Leander like a chair. They helped, spreading my ass cheeks wide, and then Leander's huge knob was there at my anus.

Being fucked by Janus there several times had stretched me. But Janus always used copious amounts of lube and stretched me carefully each time.

Leander reached around and stroked my clit. I couldn't describe his touch. He didn't just stroke me; he masterfully commanded my pleasure with his touch. I came in seconds, contracting, and then all my muscles went loose after they spasmed.

And he shoved up my ass in that moment. I opened my mouth to holler out to high heaven and Janus thrust his cock in my mouth.

"Oh fuck," Milo said, falling to his knees on the ground in front of us. And then he jutted upwards, cock in hand so he could feed it into my cunt.

I cried out around Janus's cock and he only thrust deeper down my throat, choking me.

I was pinned like a butterfly, impaled by all three of them at once.

I screamed around Janus's cock, too full, too much sensation assaulting me at once. I wasn't sure I could take it.

"I wanna fuck you till it hurts, baby," Leander said, warm chest against my back, voice in my ear. "I'm not a nice master. I want to fuck you till there's nothing left but us filling you up. I want to fuck you till all you can think about is when you can get our dick in you again. I'll fuck you till I'm your obsession. Your idol. Your god. Your everything."

26

LITTLE PLUS SIGN

His fingers at my sex massaged my swollen clit against Milo's long, firm cock thrusting inside and I shuddered, spasming as oh, *oh—*

My back shook and then my hips were quaking. My head rolled back, as far as it could with Janus's cock moving in and out of my mouth.

"That's right. Fucking give yourself up to it, baby," Leander said. "Little whores loved to be fucked in all their holes at once and you're Daddy's best little whore."

He slapped my pussy and I came harder, then his hips were dragging me up and down on his cock. He was so huge in my ass, I couldn't take him, but I was, *oh I was—*

He slapped my pussy again, and again, a spasm rocked my body.

"Fuck, she clenches on me so good when you do that," Milo said. "She's so goddamn tight. Tighter than my fist. Tighter than anything I ever felt before. I don't know how long I can hold out—"

"You'll fucking hold," Leander said. "Because we aren't

filling her up only to empty her again so quick. I want her to get a good feel for us. I want her to get used to this. If she keeps behaving like a brat this will be her permanent position every time we're back in this fucking hotel room.

He slapped my pussy again. Again, I clenched on Milo and howled around Janus, who was fucking my mouth deep—then pulling back *just* in time before I ran out of breath so I could gulp another. I guess he'd decided to tap into his inner sadist after all.

"Fuck, and the way she quivers," Milo said.

"You can't imagine what her mouth feels like," Janus hissed, and his voice sounded funny, high-pitched like he was out of breath.

"Well, I'm watching. It looks fucking amazing. Just like I can feel Leander's dick in her ass because I've never felt anything this tight or amazing or soft or— Oh Jesus, oh Jesus—"

"Hold it, you randy bastard," Leander growled, fingers digging into my hips. God, he was splitting me wide open from behind. I scrambled for something to hold onto. And found Janus's ass. It would do. I dug into his ass with my fingernails and he only fucked my face more furiously.

"You're ours now," Leander growled, the hand not on my pussy going to tweak my nipple. My feet hit the floor and then I lifted up and down, fucking him and Janus too. Which only riled them up even more. And they took back over.

They started fucking me in tandem, both thrusting and pulling out at once. All the while, Leander's hand was at my pussy. I shook with pleasure and sucked sloppily at Janus's cock until he took my head and jaw in his hands to fuck me the way he needed to.

They all used me like their toy and I came so fucking hard,

I almost blacked out. Or whited out, more like, because the pleasure twined into exhilarating light splitting outwards from my body, from my sternum up through my scalp and out through my fingertips and then I was—

I was *there*.

In that magical space.

It was quiet.

And so, so peaceful.

"Let it flow through you," Leander commanded, and I did.

Pleasure wracked me and I let it flow up and down my body, through one fingertip to the next and into the next.

I whimpered and cried my pleasure and our bodies slapped and sweated.

When Milo finally swore, "Fuck, I can't hold it anymore, I'm gonna come," Leander snapped back, "Pull out and come on her tits."

Milo roared in what sounded like frustration but did what Leander said, pulling out of me and then fisting himself furiously.

Cum spurted in a fountain as he jacked himself once, and then came a second fountain more generous than the first. He jerked his fist and another spurt, and then another, a little less each time. Even when he was dry, he kept jerking himself, and he looked totally blissed out.

"Now you, Janus."

Janus swore and I tasted the smallest bit of cum on my tongue before he yanked out of my mouth and spilled the rest on my breasts.

Leander rubbed their combined cum into my chest in that way he liked to do, like it was the most expensive of lotions. I knew later he'd shower me off with just as much attention.

It was so dirty, the cum of two men marking my chest, with Leander still balls-deep up my anus. I shivered and quivered. Then Leander's hand at my pussy started massaging me deep in that way of his again. I squealed and Leander put his hand back on my throat, just like he had at the beginning.

He lifted up so that his mouth was at my ear. "You're mine, sweet baby. I'll fuck this ass and mark you as many times as it takes for you to get the picture. Do you understand me?" His grip at my throat squeezed and I clenched around his cock in my ass.

"Yes," I whispered.

"Yes, what?" He squeezed again.

Fresh wetness gushed in my pussy. "Yes, *Daddy*."

"That's fucking right. Yes, Daddy. Now Daddy's going to fuck his little girl like she deserves. Is *that* understood?"

"Yes, Daddy," I whispered, my heart thumping.

"Daddy's going to fuck you hard and rougher than you've ever had it. Can my baby girl handle that?" His grip on my neck squeezed even tighter, and for the first time, I felt my air start to cut off.

"Yes, Daddy," I whispered through the air supply I had.

"Good." He released my throat. And then, his voice low and deep, "Hold on to something."

Then he grabbed me and thrust me face down on the couch. His lithe body landed on top of mine.

His cock had come out of my ass during the transition, but he grabbed my ass cheeks, pulled them wide apart, and then, *oh*—!

He thrust back in without hesitation or any gentleness. And then he started fucking me like he did when he was in beast mode. Except this time he was in my ass. Thankfully, a bunch of lubricant had dripped down from my pussy into my asshole, slicking his way. And he'd stretched me so much on the couch, but still—

I grunted and reached for the arm of the couch to brace myself as he fucked me so deep into the cushions.

"Fuck me, Daddy," I cried, tears cresting in my eyes. When he fucked me like this it felt like he was cleansing me. Baptizing me in all my nooks and crannies with his staff. His rod. He did *so* comfort me. And pleasure me.

"Daddy!" I squealed and the tears rolled down my cheeks. "Oh Daddy, fuck me harder up the ass. Oh Daddy, it's so good. It's so good to be fucked by you!" My clit was so swollen that when Leander fucked me furious and deep like this, my groin ground against the soft fabric of the couch, and soon I was coming again.

"D-a-a-a-a-a-addy," I cried, stuttering with each of his punching thrusts deep in my ass.

"That's right. Cry for me. Cry for me, baby. Cry for Daddy. That's right. Such a good girl. You're such a good little girl."

I came even harder.

Then he thrust harder and deeper, faster and faster until he stilled, and cum pumped deep up my ass. He thrust more and more, and I slumped to the couch, assuming we were done.

But you know what they say about assuming...

Because Leander immediately flipped me over, cum spilling out of my asshole. He flipped me over so I was on my back. Then he dragged me to the edge of the couch and dropped to his knees. Was he going to fuck me like Milo had even though he'd just come? He was still hard.

Instead, though, he dropped his mouth to my pussy.

And started to kiss me... there.

They'd only done this a few times, and never Leander before. Always Janus.

But Jesus, when Leander started doing with his tongue

what he usually did with his fingers? It was like my pussy turned straight into heaven.

I screamed.

I clawed.

I writhed and Leander held my thighs in place with his huge, muscled arms while he continued eating me out and sending waves of wracking pleasure through my center outwards.

My legs started shaking... and didn't stop. Oh God, it was so good. Oh God, I never wanted it to stop.

My hand went for Leander's head but Janus or Milo caught it, pinning it back to the couch. I flopped backwards and cried unabashedly now, tears streaming down my face as Leander wracked my body with pleasure.

Oh fuck. *It. Just. Didn't. Stop.*

It had to stop sometime, right? He had to get tired, didn't his mouth get tired, but oh, oh, *oh, holy*—!

His tongue swiped inside my pussy, where Milo's cock had just been, and I—

"I can't take anymore, *I can't*, I- I- I- I—"

"Yes, you fucking can," Leander lifted up from my sex to say, his mouth wet with my juices.

"Yes, you can, baby," Janus chimed in. "You can take more." His voice hardened. "And you will."

Leander's mouth was back at it, suckling on me, suckling so hard, pulsing my sex with his tongue—

"Oh my God, I can't—" I whined, legs shaking even more as I writhed back and forth, testing Leander's hold on my thighs.

"Help me hold her," Leander growled. "And get at those nipples. We exhaust her with pleasure now."

"Wait, what?" I looked up in alarm. But Milo and Janus were there, gazing down with intensity.

"Just look at our cum staining her tits," Milo said. Then he reached down, grabbed my nipple, and twisted hard.

I came, so trained to come from that particular move, especially when my nipples were so extremely sensitive like they were now. I howled. Janus held a hand over my mouth.

"Look how luscious her tits are. They're bouncy and luscious as fuck." Milo sounded awed.

I just writhed against Leander's torturous mouth one second… and tried to pull away from him the next.

But he didn't let me go. He tortured me with my orgasms. For half an hour more. Then longer still. Until I lost track. Until I'd come so many times I was limp. But still he made my center pulse and sting with pleasure

I wept and came and my legs shook as *yet again* he wrung another peak from my exhausted body.

"Have you had enough?" Leander asked. His voice was rough as he lifted up from between my thighs and swiped at his glistening mouth with his forearm.

I could only blink up at him dazedly. My stomach spasmed hard at the cool air against my swollen pussy.

"I think you've finally fucked her brains out," Milo grinned, hand on his hard cock. He'd taken a seat on the edge of the bed for the show. I blinked blearily just enough to register Janus on the bed behind him, watching me but not touching himself.

"Come on," Janus said, standing up. "She's exhausted. Let's get her a bath and then into bed."

"Too tired." At least that was what I meant to get out.

"That's some lovely gibberish, baby," Leander said, his voice husky and suddenly soft. He'd been so hard all night, I blinked up at him in confusion.

But he just bent down and kissed my forehead. "Such a good girl," he whispered. "Such a good, good girl."

I leaned into his chest and basked in his praise. God, I was exhausted. It felt so good to close my eyes. Leander petted my hair and kept whispering over and over what a good girl I was.

I glowed and drifted... only blinking awake a couple times in the bath as big warm hands held and bathed me. And then again when the guys laid me in bed. My eyes were shut fast when their warm bodies climbed in on both sides of me.

How could they take me from such kinky adrenaline highs and then to...*this?* The gentle washing and the cuddling as we slept? As if they were two sides of the same coin? Tears wet my eyes as I fell into sleep, overwhelmed by love for the strong men surrounding me.

Which made it all the more devastating when I woke in the middle of the night.

I stared at the ceiling, having to pee. Then, just like I had all week, I crept out down the bottom of the bed—and not a one of them moved. I didn't know whether to love or hate that they were all such heavy sleepers. I tiptoed over to the large closet to dig through my bag. The emergency contraceptive box was at the very bottom of my suitcase. All but forgotten.

I snatched it out and clutched it to my chest.

Then clicked the closet light off and hurried over to the bathroom, squeezing my eyes shut as I locked the door and it clicked.

My hands shook as I pulled the little plastic pregnancy tube out of the discreet pink and brown polka dot pencil box I'd bought on Etsy. I unwrapped it and peed on the stick.

Three minutes later, I was shaking my head at a little *plus* sign.

"No," I whispered, feeling nauseated again. "Oh hell no."

I had to stop and breathe hard, in and out several times, but I managed to keep whatever was left in my stomach down.

It didn't stop the panic from taking over the rest of my body.

A baby.

A *baby.*

I thought of Leander calling *me* baby all night. Then blinked and shook my head hard.

I'd known before tonight even began that it had been a short bubble of escape. A night out of time. But the night was over. And however amazing it had been, and no matter the heights the guys had taken to me to...

I looked down at my Fitbit on my arm. *Four thirty a.m.*

It was officially morning now. The night was over. Time to be an adult. As much as we might like to play in our scenes, I wasn't a little girl anymore.

For God's sake, I was going to be a mother!

My hands shook as I shoved the pee stick back in the pencil box. I certainly couldn't go leaving the evidence behind in the trash.

A mother.

Fuck! I didn't know much, but I did know one thing—I wouldn't be like my parents. I'd never put religion or any other thing above my child. The kid would always come first. I shivered, remembering Leander's voice. *I'll fuck you till I'm your obsession. Your idol. Your god. Your everything.*

He would become my everything if I stayed.

But I would never be his. A fist twisted my guts.

And this little baby, what would they be to him? Or Janus? My hand drifted to my belly. Was it even possible to know which of them was the father? Horrified, I shook my head firmly.

Some things just couldn't be risked.

Mind made up, I tiptoed back into the other room, grabbed my phone and one of my bags that had just enough to get me home. I froze and held my breath when one of the guys shifted in bed. But then they settled again.

Still, I didn't breathe out until I'd opened the hotel door and shut it behind me again. Slipping my flats on, I fled.

Away from the twins. Away from Milo. Away from my first loves. My first lovers. The only men I could ever imagine—

I sobbed as I ran.

But I didn't stop or turn back.

27

WHEN SHE RUNS

I smashed the down button on the elevator.

"Come on, come on," I muttered, bouncing up and down in my anxiety to get the hell out of here. Now that I'd made my decision, I was resolved. It had been insane, losing myself this summer. I needed to go back, hole up, and—

My hand fell to my stomach and tears popped out of my eyes. I needed to go back home and figure out what the hell to do next.

"Where do you think you're going?"

Oh shit. Even without turning around I knew it was Leander. Fuck. Fuck fuck fuck.

The elevator pinged open and I ran inside and slammed the close button. I was close, so close to getting the hell out of there. I just needed to think, I needed to think, and I couldn't do that around—

But it was adorable thinking I could get the elevator doors to shut before Leander's furious strides down the hallway would bring him to me. His strong arm forced its way inside the doors before they shut and my stomach sank even as my heart soared.

Because some foolish part inside of me still hoped he could make it all better. That if I just laid down all my defenses, my Daddies would make it all better.

Which only showed what a fool I was.

Leander glared at me and I'd never seen him more furious. He was usually so good at controlling his emotions, but apparently waking up in bed only to find me gone had made him one grumpy boy.

"I thought we just went over this." He put a hand over my head on the elevator wall and leaned into me, not touching my body. "You. Do. Not. Run. Ever."

I wanted to sink into him. I wanted to curl my body against his, nod and say, yes, Daddy. Of course.

But that was before, and this was now. There was a pregnancy test in my bag with a plus sign.

So I shoved away from the wall of the elevator and out from underneath the magnetic hold of his gaze.

"It's over," I said roughly, choking back my tears. "This was always just temporary and we all knew it. One day you're going to toss me away and find some new..." I glared over my shoulder at him, "*...publicist.*"

His jaw went tight. "That's not fucking fair. You're nothing like Geena and we don't treat you anything like her."

My heart wanted to believe it. But life had taught me differently. Men could say nice words. My dad used to talk so sweet about my mama when he was up in front of the congregation. About how he loved her like God loved the church and other beautiful words.

But when push came to shove, he wanted her in his kitchen doing his laundry not saying a word back to him, never going out, raising his babies—

Baby.

"I'm leaving."

The elevator pinged again and the doors opened at the lobby.

Right into the bodies of Janus and Milo. "What's going on?" Janus asked, eyes on Leander. "Why'd she run?"

Milo alone was looking at me. "Are you okay, honey?"

"She's coming back up with us and she's going to finally tell us what the hell is going on in that head of hers," Leander said.

Janus nodded, stepping on the elevator and crowding me backwards so that I had no choice but to back up to the corner. Milo followed him in and the elevator doors closed.

"Apparently, she didn't learn her lesson about running and not talking to us," Leander said, his voice low and dangerous.

"Leander," Milo warned.

"Enough," Leander snapped. "She's going to learn one way or another. No matter how red her ass gets learning the lesson."

"No!" I objected, and all three men looked at me in surprise at my outburst. But I wasn't standing down. I glared at every single one of them. "None of you is laying a fucking hand on me."

The tears I couldn't keep back finally exploded over the rims of my eyes and flooded down my face.

But I'd had enough. Enough of their cocky attitudes and just— Enough!

"You wanna know why I'm running?" I asked, laughing bitterly through my tears. "Fine." I reached in the one bag I'd brought and rustled around, then when I couldn't find it, I dramatically dumped it all out on the floor of the elevator right as it pinged on our floor.

That didn't stop me. I kept rifling through the few pairs of underwear I'd packed and lip gloss and— There!

I held up the positive pregnancy test in triumph, then yanked off the little protective plastic cover so they could see the results. I skewered Leander and Janus with my gaze.

"One of you barbaric bastards knocked me up."

28

YOU DON'T KNOW THE MEANING OF THE WORD

Leander took a step backward like he'd been struck, shaking his head *no* back and forth. But Janus, Janus got the biggest smile on his face.

He immediately dropped down and started shoving crap back into my bag.

Milo just stared at all of us, his mouth dropping open in an O of surprise. Frankly, I'd expected all of them to act like that.

I looked back at Leander, who'd suddenly crossed his arms over his chest. The elevator had started beeping from Milo pressing the Door Open button while Janus gathered the rest of the things and shoved them in my bag.

Leander snatched the pregnancy test out of my hand and looked at it closer. "How do we know it's real?"

"Jesus fuck, you goddamn idiot," Janus looked up from where he was perched on the ground. "Of course it's real. She was a virgin."

"So she says," Leander said cooly.

And if I wasn't so tired and emotional, I would have slapped the bastard.

"If you weren't paying attention, you mean bastard, I was

trying to *leave.*" I shoved Leander hard in the chest and then pushed my way through Leander and Janus, who had just stood up. I yanked my bag from Janus as I went.

"So it isn't ours after all," Leander said, and he sounded like a stranger. "She's exactly like Geena, fucking other men behind our back."

The obsessive man demanding I stay only minutes ago was completely gone. It hurt more than it should, even though I knew this was where it would all eventually lead. They'd go cold and hurt me, and I was right to have tried to leave first.

I shrugged and tried to be as ice cold as he was as I glared back at him. "I guess that's the only explanation you'll accept."

"All of you shut up," Janus said. "And let's get back to our hotel room."

I huffed out a laugh. "Fat chance. I'm outta here." I hiked my bag up on my shoulder and then I started down the hallway. If they could take the stairs, so could I.

"Don't you dare go anywhere when you have our baby in you," Janus said, arm winding through mine and stopping me before I could go even one step.

"It's not our baby," Leander growled. "She was taking birth control—"

A group of people passed by with luggage, obviously early morning checkouts. But they slowed down when they passed by what was most obviously a *scene.*

Then I heard the whisper, "Hey, isn't that—" I didn't catch all of it but I did hear *Mavros.*

Shit. As of the moment I was still officially their publicist. I breathed out hard. "Fine," I hissed. "I'll come back to the room to talk." Janus looked triumphant and I pointed in his face. "It doesn't mean I'm staying."

He nodded and all but dragged me back towards the hotel suite.

My brain spun like a tilt-a-whirl all the way there, and yet it still wasn't enough time to get my wits straight before we were back in the room and they were bombarding me with questions.

"How soon can we get a DNA test?" Leander asked, right as Janus, who'd never let go of my arm, reached to cradle my tummy.

I yanked back from him. "I'm not getting a DNA test," I said indignantly. "If you can't believe me that I haven't had sex with anyone else, then you don't need to be part of my kid's life. Jesus," I said, throwing my hands up in the air. "You think I have to go find *more* men to sleep with! You all just fucked every hole I have at the same time. Who do you think I am?"

But it was obvious staring into Leander's stony face who he thought I was. Geena. Or one of the other incalculable number of women they'd done this with before.

And I'd thought I was special. That what was between us was different.

"We know you aren't like anyone else. You're different," Janus said, and I just rolled my eyes. "Special."

"Ha," I said right into his face.

But Janus wasn't backing down. He grabbed my cheeks, gripping my face as he forced me to look at him. "Ignore my fucking ignorant brother and listen."

His chameleon eyes sparkled silver. "This is the most exciting news of my entire life. You've made me the happiest man alive. You're going to have our baby, honey. I love you." He bent his forehead against mine. "You love me." He said it firmly, as if to remind me. "It's okay if this had you running scared. I understand."

"I fucking don't!" Leander bit out. "It's as much of a betrayal as any woman we've ever known. And to me this looks like a trap to catch a couple of celebrities. Even if it is real, as soon as we started taking you raw-dog, what? Did you replace the birth control with sugar pills?"

I jerked away from Janus, fury spiking in a way I'd never felt before. I flew at Leander. "You bastard!" I wanted to hit him. I wanted to make him hurt the way he was hurting me. But he caught my wrists before I could even make contact.

And then he laughed at me and it was not a nice laugh. "Oh, poor little girl. Whored yourself out to the biggest celebrity you could find and for what? I'll *get* my DNA test. And if this is indeed my runt in your belly, you'll never see a goddamn dime, I promise you that."

I wanted to scream at him.

Instead, I spat in his face.

For a second, everyone in the room froze.

And then the cruelest smile yet curled up Leander's face as he wiped my spittle from his face with his shoulder. His grip on my shoulders tightened.

"Oh, pet. We've been taking it so easy on you. You're going to be in for nine months of hell as you learn the meaning of *obedience*."

I quivered in his arms. "I hate you," I hissed.

He smiled even wider, his quicksilver eyes turning darker than I'd ever seen them. "Oh baby girl, you don't even understand the meaning of the word yet..."

or, if you prefer the ebook, Season Two will be out later this summer :)

ROCKSTAR GODS COMING JULY 1ST, 2022. Read on for a sneak peek.

JOIN MY NEWSLETTER HERE [HTTPS://WWW.STASIABLACK.COM/CONTACT] for first peeks, new release news, ARCs, and more. No spamming, ever!

SNEAK PEEK OF ROCKSTAR GODS

Chapter 1

HIM

They always say yes to my deals.

Always.

I'm careful who I pick, you see.

I only bring the most broken, desperate, and gullible mortals to the crossroads.

That's not to say that I'm not fair. I am. Scrupulously so.

I offer them a deal but apply zero compulsion for them to say yes. They do that all on their own. Every single time.

...until her.

When she got to the crossroads, she looked around, crouched low, and barked, "Where the hell am I?" Then she looked at me. "And who the fuck are you?"

Plenty have been surprised by their sudden appearance at my shadowy abode, but still, no one said no to the deal.

So what was I supposed to do?

Thousands of years, hundreds of thousands of crossroads deals and so many souls collected that I was more powerful than ever—

And then some mortal says *no* to *me*? And not just no but *fuck no*, I believe were her exact words?

I was a god, she a mere mortal! Who was she to say no to me and deny me her soul? She had nothing else and I offered her *everything.*

So, I thought, having nothing, perhaps she simply didn't have enough to lose yet. It could happen sometimes with the young, I supposed, though none had ever surprised me like this before.

So I gave her the world.

Knowing that one day I'd be back.

And I'd make her beg me on her knees for a deal.

Oh yes I'd make her crawl on her face in the dirt.

Because while mortals had *absolute free will* to say no to my deals, it didn't mean I wouldn't make them pay for it.

Or ever stop hunting them for their soul.

Chapter 2

MACE

Sweat poured down my brow as the grand piano I sat at was engulfed in stage light from above. The crowd roared as I began to play the recognizable notes that intro'd our most recent hit. It was a ballad I'd written that had been lighting up radio stations and streaming platforms. Our band, *Faust*, was more popular than ever.

I looked over at *her* as I struck the keys harder, leaning into the piano as the music rang out from my instrument.

Then Bishop, our lead singer moved up on the mike like he was giving it head. I sagged back on my bench, glaring up at him. It was unfair that such a goddamned asshole had been given a honeyed voice from the gods.

And I detested how good he sounded singing my lyrics.

I gave you up before calling you mine.

Oh baby, not this time.

Not this time.

I glanced towards her again, wondering if she had any clue it was *me* singing to her. She was oblivious, though, lost in the song as she started drumming the symbols to make a rushing sound as Bishop looked back at her and winked.

That, she saw, naturally, and grinned.

I glared at them and leaned harder into my next chord than was strictly necessary. No one noticed. The crowd was singing along to my words as the chorus broke out.

Now we're past the point of no return.

So tuuuuuuuurn with me

and we'll tuuuuurn in ecstasy

oh retuuuuuurn to me

I'd swear I'd never leg go,

if she would only—

tuuuuuurn her eyes...

on me.

Bishop pulled back the mic for Luna's dramatic drum solo break. I'd written that in just for her.

Luna.

The light in our darkness. The moon in our night.

The band would have imploded years ago if not for her. She didn't know how much we all relied on her.

All our egos together? Ha. No way we would've made it. Bishop and me alone would have torn each other apart. And that's not even mentioning Cash, who's ego could fill a whole building all on his own. He's positive he's god's gift to women, to our band, to lead-guitaring, to music and humanity in general.

But Luna's calm, mediating presence always kept us in check. Kept us music. On the road touring without too many mishaps. Wash, rinse, repeat. That had been life for the last seven years.

A good life. Apart from putting up with Bishop and all his bullshit... And there had been offers over the years to leave... But leaving the band meant leaving *her*, and that was something I just couldn't bring myself to do.

Especially lately.

Why was I still denying myself what I wanted? What I'd swear *she* wanted too, by the look I sometimes caught in her eye?

Because I mean, it was an ignorant fucking deal I agreed to all those years ago.

Story of my life, I thought as the stage lights briefly darkened so I could move back to the electric keyboard for our last song.

Me and making bad fucking deals I'd regret for the rest of my life. I shivered even as the lights went back up again.

Part of me still didn't want to believe that night after graduation had been real.

But—as Luna went crazy on the drums and Bishop started sing-screaming into the microphone in a way that had the fans going nuts again—it was like I was back there.

I revisited it often enough in my dreams to be able to recall every detail even though it had been near on eight years now.

I'd made a desperate plea to the night, and then fallen asleep in my car. After what had happened that afternoon at the house, I just wanted to be anywhere but home.

Then I woke up and I was... *there*.

I'd never had the words to describe it. Ironic, since words were kinda my whole gig. I was the main lyricist of the group, except for when Bishop got a hair up his ass and decided he was a song-writer again.

But yeah, that night, that place.

It was dark, pitch-black out. Except there was still some light, somehow. I never did decide where it was coming from. It was dark, black out all around so you couldn't see much except some fog and two roads crossing in the middle of freaking *nowhere*. I lived in the city and there was no land like that anywhere I'd ever seen—flat, empty, no lights in the distance. It was inhuman, and cold, and wrong.

And then *he* was there, or maybe I should call him an *it*? It had a male voice but it was all shadows, only *sort of* in the shape of a man. The shadows kept shifting, no matter how I squinted.

When it spoke, ice ran through my veins.

But then it—*he*— knew everything about me, and my situation, and even what had happened that afternoon.

He said he'd heard my plea and was there to help.

He would be happy to kill my father for me.

In that moment, I'd forgotten all the strangeness of the place. In my desperation and sudden hope, all I could ask was, "Can you make it hurt?"

And I felt more than saw the shadow smile. "I can most definitely see to that."

When I woke up and shook off the sleep of the night, I dove home only to find police already there.

They were notifying my mother that my father had died in a car crash. He didn't die on impact, they said. They were so sorry to tell us, but he'd gone over a cliff. He'd been trapped inside for twenty minutes while the car caught fire and had slowly burned to death.

I kept my face blank as the police finished telling us the gory details. And I gave my mom a supportive hug as she collapsed into my arms.

But I was smiling into her hair.

Apparently, a deal was a deal. And at the time, losing my eternal soul just didn't seem that important.

ALSO BY STASIA BLACK

Reverse Harem Romances

Marriage Raffle Series

Theirs To Protect [https://geni.us/Th2Pr-EN-w]

Theirs To Pleasure [https://geni.us/Th2Pl-EN-w]

Theirs To Wed [https://geni.us/Th2We-EN-w]

Theirs To Defy [https://geni.us/Th2De-EN-w]

Theirs To Ransom [https://geni.us/Th2Ra-EN-w]

Marriage Raffle Boxset Part 1 [https://geni.us/MaRaBx-EN-w]

Marriage Raffle Boxset Part 2 [https://geni.us/MaRaBx-2-EN-w]

Freebie

Their Honeymoon [https://BookHip.com/QHCQDM]

Dark Contemporary Romances

Breaking Belles Series

Elegant Sins [https://geni.us/ElSi-EN-w]

Beautiful Lies [https://geni.us/BeLi-EN-w]

Opulent Obsession [https://geni.us/OpOb-EN-w]

Inherited Malice [https://geni.us/InMa-EN-w]

Delicate Revenge [https://geni.us/DeRe-EN-w]

Lavish Corruption

Dark Mafia Series

Innocence [https://geni.us/Innocence-EN-w]

Awakening [https://geni.us/Awakening-EN-w]

Queen of the Underworld [https://geni.us/QuOfThUn-EN-w]

Persephone & Hades (Box Set) [https://geni.us/InBx-EN-w]

Beauty and the Rose Series

Beauty's Beast [https://geni.us/BeBe-EN-w]

Beauty and the Thorns [https://geni.us/BeNThTh-EN-w]

Beauty and the Rose [https://geni.us/BeNThRo-EN-w]

Billionaire's Captive (Box Set) [https://geni.us/BiCa-EN-w]

Love So Dark Series

Cut So Deep [https://geni.us/CuSDe-EN-w]

Break So Soft [https://geni.us/BrSSo-EN-w]

Love So Dark (Box Set) [https://geni.us/LoSDa-EN-w]

Stud Ranch Series

The Virgin and the Beast [https://geni.us/ThViNThBe-EN-w]

Hunter [https://geni.us/Hunter-EN-w]

The Virgin Next Door [https://geni.us/ThViNeDo-EN-w]

Reece [https://geni.us/Reece-EN-w]

Jeremiah [https://geni.us/Jeremiah-EN-w]

Taboo Series

Daddy's Sweet Girl [https://geni.us/DaSwGi-EN-w]

Hurt So Good [https://geni.us/HuSGo-EN-w]

Taboo: a Dark Romance Boxset Collection [https://geni.us/Taboo_Bx-EN-w]

Vasiliev Bratva Series

Without Remorse [https://geni.us/WiRe-EN-w]

Freebie

Indecent: A Taboo Proposal [https://geni.us/SBA-nw-cont-w]

Sci-fi Romances

Draci Alien Series

My Alien's Obsession [https://geni.us/MyAlOb-EN-w]

My Alien's Baby [https://geni.us/MyAlBa-EN-w]

My Alien's Beast [https://geni.us/MyAlBe-EN-w]

ABOUT THE AUTHOR

STASIA BLACK grew up in Texas, recently spent a freezing five-year stint in Minnesota, and now is happily planted in sunny California, which she will never, ever leave.

She loves writing, reading, listening to podcasts, and has recently taken up biking after a twenty-year sabbatical (and has the bumps and bruises to prove it). She lives with her own personal cheerleader, aka, her handsome husband, and their teenage son. Wow. Typing that makes her feel old. And writing about herself in the third person makes her feel a little like a nutjob, but ahem! Where were we?

Stasia's drawn to romantic stories that don't take the easy way out. She wants to see beneath people's veneer and poke into their dark places, their twisted motives, and their deepest desires. Basically, she wants to create characters that make readers alternately laugh, cry ugly tears, want to toss their kindles across the room, and then declare they have a new FBB (forever book boyfriend).

~

Join Stasia's Facebook Group for Readers for access to deleted scenes, to chat with me and other fans and also get access to exclusive giveaways:

Stasia's Facebook Reader Group

~

Want to read an EXCLUSIVE, FREE novella, Indecent: a Taboo Proposal, that is available ONLY to my newsletter subscribers, along with news about upcoming releases, sales, exclusive giveaways, and more?

Get **Indecent: a Taboo Proposal**

When Mia's boyfriend takes her out to her favorite restaurant on their six-year anniversary, she's expecting one kind of proposal. What she didn't expect was her boyfriend's longtime rival, Vaughn McBride, to show up and make a completely different sort of offer: all her boyfriend's debts will be wiped clear. The price?

One night with her.

Website: stasiablack.com
Facebook: facebook.com/StasiaBlackAuthor
Twitter: twitter.com/stasiawritesmut
Instagram: instagram.com/stasiablackauthor
Goodreads: goodreads.com/stasiablack
BookBub: bookbub.com/authors/stasia-black

Made in the USA
Las Vegas, NV
15 May 2022